"Hilarious action adventure that will have you hunting for your snow gear. The perfect winter read!"
~HEATHER WOODHAVEN,
Novelist and Mom

"A fun romp through childhood."
~BILL MYERS,
Creator of *McGee and Me*, Best-selling Author, Award-Winning Filmmaker

"I love it. My kids think *The Water Fight Professional* should be made into a movie!"
~JILL WILLIAMSON,
Award-Winning Children's Author

"Reading *The Water Fight Professional* is more fun than licking a slug."
~JUDY COX, Children's Author

"The protagonist's offbeat profession and Angela Strong's vibrant voice make *The Water Fight Professional* a book that young teens will eat up. Want to keep energetic boys and girls entertained for a few hours? Hand them this book."
~JEANNIE ST. JOHN TAYLOR,
Radio Host and Author/Illustrator of more than thirty books

THE SNOWBALL

FIGHT PROFESSIONAL

Written by
Angela Ruth Strong

Illustrated by
Jim Strong

Ashberry Lane

Published in association with the literary agency of Wordserve
Literary Group, www.wordserveliterary.com

ISBN 978-1-941720-13-4

Cover design by Miller Media Solutions
Illustrations by Jim Strong
Title font by Kimberly Geswein

FICTION / Middle Grade

To Caitlin—

My best Christmas gift ever

Every good and perfect gift is from above.
James 1:17

Hattie!
Merry
Christmas!

Love
Rhode
Kru

Chapter One:

Rocking in a Winter Wonderland

"I hate snow." My dad hunched over the steering wheel, eyes squinting out the windshield, doing a pretty good impersonation of The Grinch.

"Dad," I admonished, "how can you say that? It's great ammunition."

"It's not so great for visibility."

My fingers curled around my new fifty-foot range snowball launcher. It had just come in the mail, and I couldn't wait to try it out. A little Christmas gift to myself—paid for with some of the money I, Joey Michaels, had saved during my water-fighting days.

Unfortunately, a two-hour trip up into the mountains stood between me and sheer snowball-launching bliss. The good news was that, when we got there, the ground would be covered with a blanket of marvelous snow.

By five o'clock, the sun had already set for the day. The way our headlights lit the snowflakes, it looked as if we were traveling through space at light speed.

1

It made me want to pretend we were in a spaceship and my snowball launcher was actually a laser blaster. I aimed at my nine-year-old sister, Christine, and made a laser blaster sound. "Buzzoinka."

"Mom, Joey is pretending to shoot me with his snowball launcher."

"Laser blaster." I held up a finger. "And I think I accidentally fried your brain because you sound like a dumdum."

"Mom!" Christine screeched again, practically proving my point.

"Mom!" I echoed. If you can't beat 'em, join 'em. "Christine is tattling!"

The car slipped on the road. Christine flew sideways into me. My tummy flipped like I was back in gymnastics, and Mom screamed. That was cool. Not the part where Christine flew into me but the part where we slid toward the edge of the road and the river below.

Once, my school bus had spun 360 degrees on ice. I still wish I'd been bumper hitching behind it at the time, but at least we were two hours late for school that day. Best school day ever.

Mom fanned her face like she couldn't get enough oxygen. She did that a lot, whether we were careening toward the edge of a cliff or she was discovering I'd been

2

wearing the same pair of socks for a week.

Dad was a little cooler. He muttered under his breath as he regained control of the car.

Christine pushed away from me like we were sitting under mistletoe or something. "Eww … gross."

Apparently she cared more about her proximity to me than her proximity to sudden death.

"Okay." Mom caught her breath and turned down the radio as if that would help Dad keep the wheels on the road.

I would rather she had left the volume up because I liked barking along with the dogs to the tune of "Jingle Bells."

"Kids, let's play the Peace-on-Earth Game." AKA the Quiet Game. Her favorite game.

"If you wanted peace on earth, Mom, you shouldn't have let Joey spend his money on another weapon."

I hugged the snowball launcher close and whispered, "Don't listen to her, boy. We are so excited to have you in the family."

Mom turned around to face us. "Sweetie, it's not a weapon. It's athletic equipment. Yukigassen is a competitive snowball-fighting sport in Japan that is spreading around the world. It might even be in the Olympics one day."

3

She'd recited my argument perfectly. I should be a salesman when I grew up … if I didn't make it as a pro Yukigassen player.

The whites of Christine's eyes flashed in the dark as she rolled them at me. "Dad, I can't believe you let him spend all his money on himself."

"Not all my money." I had six bucks left.

"Well, I spent *my* money on Christmas presents for others."

Sure she did. At the grocery store around the corner. I bet she got me Q-Tips again so I could clean out my ears to better hear her lectures.

Dad cleared his throat. "Joe *made* gifts this year."

I smiled my smug, middle-school smile. Now that I was in 7th grade, I got to take this class called "shop." I know, it sounded like a class Mom and Christine would attend to prepare for the day-after-Thanksgiving sales, but actually we got to use manly power tools in there. I made a pegboard game for Dad, a casserole holder for Mom, a birdhouse for Christine, a guitar pick for Grandpa, and a picture frame with our last name engraved on it for Grandma.

Christine crossed her arms and sat back. "Humph."

Mom clapped her hands. "Since you've all lost the Peace-on-Earth Game, let's take turns saying what we are most looking forward to this Christmas."

Dad tapped his brakes and we slowed for a narrow bridge. "I'm looking forward to getting through this storm and parking the car."

I pressed my lips together to keep from saying, "Bah, humbug," and patted Dad on the shoulder instead. He'd be a different person when we got to his parents' house and he was able to sneak some of Grandma's goodies behind Mom's back. That's what he was really looking forward to. Hopefully he'd swipe me a couple peanut butter reindeer and some peppermint fudge while he was at it.

"Yeah." Mom was clueless about Dad's sweet tooth. "I'm looking forward to helping out with the Living Nativity. Are you sure you don't want to play the part of Joseph, Joey? You have the perfect name for it."

Dad's teeth glinted in the rearview mirror as he cracked his first smile since we'd climbed into the car.

I smiled back. "How about I play a shepherd? Then I could use the hook of my staff for a slingshot."

A passing car illuminated Mom's worry wrinkle between her eyebrows that only appeared when she was looking at me. "Never mind. Christine, what are you excited about?"

Christine flipped her hair so it slapped me in the face.

5

"Ice-skating. Can I get one of those fancy ice-skating outfits?"

I imagined myself commandeering a Zamboni and chasing her around the ice rink, but Mom must not have been imagining the same thing. "You want to become a figure skater? We could sign you up for lessons and—"

"No." Dad turned up the speed on the windshield wipers. "Not unless she wants to give up her dance lessons. Or singing lessons. Or piano lessons."

"Please, Daddy?"

Dad was usually a sucker for Christine's "Please, Daddy," but it didn't override his mental calculator this time. "Christine, if you want to take all your Christmas gifts back and use the money to pay for your own lessons, that would be fine."

Ouch. Turning the holiday into a business transaction? That was extreme, even for Dad.

Mom's head turned Dad's way. He was getting "the look" even though it was too dark to see it.

Dad must have known. "So … Joe. What about you? What are you looking forward to?"

Besides hoping that I got an arctic snow shield under the Christmas tree? I chose not to speak the idea aloud in case it hurt my snowball launcher's feelings. The poor guy was probably still smarting from Christine's

6

rejection of him. I looked down at the sleek new addition to my life.

Should I name him? He was kind of a pet.

Speaking of pets … "I'm excited to see Grandma's new husky puppies."

Grandma bred huskies. I'd always wanted one, and Dad said I could have one of my own when I saved enough money. But how many snowball launchers could I buy for the price of one of Grandma's husky puppies? More than thirty. It would be a while before I got a dog.

"Oh, me too," Christine said.

I smiled at her. She was a girly girl, but at least we both agreed that Grandma's puppies were the coolest things on earth.

"Look at you two getting along." Mom twisted all the way around to look at us, though I doubted she could actually see anything in the dark. "Are we on 34th Street? Because this is a miracle."

"Ha ha." I humored Mom. That was as good as her jokes got.

Dad chuckled for real. "It's not 34th Street, but we are almost to Easy Street. Just one more curve, then we will leave this river behind."

I looked out the window toward the side of the road that dropped away over an embankment into inky blackness. Not quite as inviting a scene as it had been last summer on our rafting trip.

"Over the river and through the woods," Mom sang.

It had taken more than an hour for her to burst into song. A new record.

Christine and I shook our heads sadly at each other. At least we were continuing to agree on things. This might turn out to be a peaceful Christmas after all.

"To Grandmother's house we—"

A deer leaped in front of Dad's headlights.

"—Whoa!" Mom changed the lyrics, though she wasn't overreacting this time.

Tires screeched.

I jolted forward then swayed violently from side to side as our vehicle fishtailed.

Christine's shriek pierced the air.

I gripped my snowball launcher tighter and ground my teeth together. We were going to be okay. Dad was a safe driver. Just because it looked like we were headed for the edge of the road—

The car jumped as one of the rear tires slid off the edge and slammed the bottom of our car on cement.

Chapter Two:

I'm Dreaming of a Whitewater Christmas

This couldn't be happening. I must have fallen asleep on the car ride and was having a nightmare. I should have known I was dreaming when Christine and I started to get along. Any minute I would wake up and—

"Hang on!" Dad yelled.

I grabbed the door handle as the car slid along the side of the road, one tire hanging over the edge, sparks shooting up behind us, the chemical smell of burning rubber singeing my nose hairs. Having a dad yell in fear was enough to make anybody wet his pants.

As if in slow motion, Dad wrestled with the steering wheel.

I'd done this on my bike before—when one tire just didn't make it over a lip on the street. I usually wiped out. But we weren't on a bike. We were in a car.

And my dad was driving. Strong, stable, no-nonsense Dad.

The steering wheel jerked out of my father's hands.

The front tire on Mom's side leaped over the edge to join the back one as we kept sliding.

Dad and I threw our weight away from the girls. Could we scramble out our doors to safety? Could we pull Mom and Christine after us in time?

Christine reached for me. "Joey!" she shrieked. She shouted my name all the time, but never asking for help.

If I didn't do something, she might never have the chance to shout my name again. I dropped my snowball launcher and grabbed her arms, scared to take off our seat belts, but scared not to at the same time. We had to get out of the car.

I couldn't see anything except snow in the headlights. Deceptively serene.

Our ragged breaths echoed loudly in the stillness.

The car tipped. Slipped. Gravel crunched again. Rocks splashed into the river below.

Our headlights swung down as the vehicle dove off the road.

Ground rushed up to meet us. We could only see what was directly spotlighted by our headlights.

Grass. Bushes. Rocks. Water.

A *crunch* … then darkness.

My head snapped back against my headrest. The seat belt ground into my gut.

10

Christine's fingernails clawed my flesh. She didn't relent even though we'd stopped moving.

My pants were wet. Had I really peed?

No. Urine would be warm. This liquid stung like an ice cube. River water.

"We're in the river!" I shouted.

Maybe this was when they would wake me up.

But no. They were all in just as much shock. Because our situation was real.

The car rocked in the waves, making more of a boat-against-the-dock sound than a car-on-the-road sound. Beyond that was the dull roar of whitewater.

A bright spot of light appeared on the ceiling. Mom's flashlight app on her phone.

The light bounced around the car, blinding me for a second.

"Are you kids all right?" she asked.

I couldn't see much in the dark, so I did a mental check of my body parts. My spine throbbed the way it normally did after a day of riding roller coasters in Salt Lake City and spending the night in a tent at the campground next to the amusement park, but the only real pain came from the icy puddle of water starting to creep its way up my legs. "I think so." I unsnapped my seat belt, detached myself from Christine's clutch, pulled

11

my legs up to the dry seat, and pressed my nose to the frigid window pane.

"We're going to be all right, kids. We're going to be all right." Dad's voice sounded calm.

How could Dad be so sure? I didn't even know if we were floating. Or sinking. Or lodged between rocks.

"I'm scared." Christine's voice quavered.

The flashlight passed across the car toward the driver's side. Mom must have handed it to Dad so she could comfort Christine.

I waited for the small circle of light to shine out the window to get a visual of our surroundings. It would be up to us men to rescue the women. My pulse pounded louder.

The small ray of light illuminated a mix of rocks and water. We weren't floating downstream yet, so that was good. We'd have to get a little wet, but we'd be able to climb across the rocks toward land.

"We have to get out of here," Dad said.

"We can do it, Dad." Because the scary part was over. But then I shoved the door open. Hard.

A gush of water poured in. The kind of water that was so cold I might as well have been zapped with the defibrillator thingies emergency workers use.

Before I knew it, I'd scrambled out onto the roof of

12

the car. But getting out of the water didn't help at all. My jeans clung to me like frost to a Popsicle.

"Christine, get up there with your brother!" Dad barked.

She tried to follow. I know this not because I saw her, but because her screams grew louder.

I squinted, forcing my pupils to adjust.

There. A small hand over the edge of the roof.

"Can you get her, Joe?"

Shivering, I crawled close enough to grasp her fingers and pull.

She slithered onto the roof with me like a baby penguin at the zoo would climb the rocks. Except honestly, the better analogy would have to include Antarctica. In the dead of winter.

I huddled close to her for the little bit of body heat radiating through her mostly dry shirt.

She didn't get grossed out this time.

Dad's head appeared as he climbed out onto an adjacent rock. He swung the light toward me for a moment before shining the light on Mom and reaching back down for her. "Stay right there, Joe."

No worries about that. I'd pretty much frozen in place.

Mom's head appeared. Then disappeared. "Oww …"

13

"Mommy!" Christine cried out.

Dad's head disappeared.

"What's wrong?" I yelled to Dad.

He didn't answer immediately. Or maybe he did, but I couldn't hear him over the roar of the river.

Both their heads popped back up, Mom's arm around Dad's neck this time. "She hurt her ankle," he yelled to me.

Then came another voice. "Do you need help?"

Two more beams of light made their way down the embankment toward us.

"Yes! And call 9-1-1." Dad turned his beam of light toward them.

Guys in ski jackets.

"Thank You, Jesus," I said. Answered prayer was awesome, but having God answer a prayer I forgot to pray was even better. He was looking out for me even when I haven't been good. Not even Santa Claus did that.

The car jolted beneath me. Christine and I gripped the edge of the roof before it bucked us off. It stopped just as suddenly as the movement started, though my heart continued its plunge.

All three flashlights swung our way.

"The riverbed is starting to give way," one of the guys

14

said.

That didn't sound good.

Uh, God? I forgot to pray earlier, but I'm praying now. Help!

"Here." Dad handed Mom off to the first guy that reached him. "You get her up to the road, and I'll get the kids."

Mom clung to the stranger as she hobbled away. I'd never seen her hobble before. She was usually more of a prancer.

Dad extended an arm toward us. "Take my hand, Christine."

She shook her head and gripped my shoulders tighter.

Oh boy.

"Come on, honey. The sooner you reach for me, the sooner I can get you to Grandma and Grandpa's."

She didn't budge. Except for the way she trembled.

Or maybe that was me trembling. "Go, Christine, or I'll try out my snowball launcher on you first." That might have sounded mean, but it did the job.

Christine turned her head my way as if giving me a dirty look I couldn't see, then her limbs untangled from mine.

"One, two, three," Dad counted.

She was gone. No splash, so she must have made it to the rock.

15

Without her weight, the car shifted again. As great a story as it would make, I really did not want to go surfing down the Payette River on top of a car roof. Wrong season.

I slowly scooted to a crouched position. I couldn't wait for Dad's hand or the other rescue hero to reach me. It was now or never. I focused on the small beam of light. That's where I would land. I'd just have to count down for myself. "One."

"Wait, Joe."

"Two."

"Son, let me help you."

He didn't understand. The car wasn't going to respect his timeline. "Three."

I leaped. Through the night. Not seeing, but feeling. My pulse pounded in my throat. Cool air intensified the sting of my wet pants. Gravity pulled me toward the unknown. My feet hit solid ground, and I sank onto my knees to absorb the impact just like I did on the trampoline. Except I'd landed on a slope and tipped backward, about to continue my descent.

Dad's hand shot out of the darkness and grabbed the collar of my shirt.

Safe.

"I told you to wait," he said. So much for a hug of joy

to celebrate my survival.

"I couldn't." I reached for his flashlight and swung the light toward the backseat of the car where I'd been sitting in boredom only a few minutes before.

Funny how every second in life mattered whether I realized it or not.

Making every one of those seconds count, I hung onto Dad with one hand, illuminated my snowball blaster, and grabbed it from the wreckage just as the car wobbled, groaned, and took off in a jet stream of whitewater.

Finally my father gave me the joyful hug I'd been expecting.

Chapter Three:

All I Want for Christmas is Two Front Paws

Grandpa's flannel pajamas were a little big for me, but better to trip on their long hem than have to get dressed in one of my cousin Winston's many sweater vests.

I stumbled my way to the barstool in Grandma's kitchen. "Snowman pancakes?" I asked with all the anticipation of a preschooler. That's how old I was when Grandma started making the special meal. There's just something satisfying about biting off Frosty's head.

"Yes, snowman pancakes." Grandma placed the plate in front of me.

Raisin eyes, a bacon scarf, and marshmallows below him to look like snow.

I stuffed the marshmallows all in my mouth at once before Mom could stop me.

"Joey." Mom scowled from her spot in front of the fireplace before wobbling my direction on crutches.

I grinned, enjoying the way the marshmallows had dissolved into a goo and squished between my teeth.

18

Winston pulled out a stool next to mine. "That's disgusting."

Talk about disgusting. Winston sat with perfect posture and folded his hands in his lap. The kid was supposed to be my age, but I was convinced he'd had a true-life Freaky Friday experience, and he was really a parent trapped in a kid's body. Somewhere out in adult world was my real cousin living it up as a twelve-year-old who looked like a man and got away with eating marshmallows for breakfast anytime he wanted.

"How are you feeling, Carolyn?" Grandma asked my mother.

"Merry and bright," said Mom, though she sounded more like "cranky and gloomy."

I angled my body away from her to shield my actions as I dumped syrup on the pancake man, but Mom knew me well enough to know exactly what I was doing.

She reached over my shoulder and snatched away the bottle of maple tastiness.

The action caused a crutch to slip out from under her shoulder and crash to the floor.

Mom hopped on one foot. Tipping, she put her casted foot on the ground to catch herself, and her mouth opened in a silent scream.

I blinked in surprise. I probably should have reached

19

for her, but Dad swooped in and caught her right in time.

My jaw dropped. Usually Mom danced around the house while seizing sugary snacks out of people's mouths, but now she couldn't even do it standing in place.

This was awesome! Not the Mom-being-hurt part, which I felt horrible about. Just the tasty treat quota I would reach before we went home.

"Mom," I said in my best concerned voice. "You better go lie on the couch before you hurt yourself."

"Ohh …" she moaned, handing the syrup across the counter to Grandma—as if that would keep it out of my reach. "What am I going to do?"

"Come on, honey." Dad led her back toward the fireplace.

"I can't go skiing now. Or ice-skating. Goodness, I can't even go shopping to get us all clothes or toothbrushes."

That would be tough on her. But hey, it meant more syrup for me. I grabbed the syrup Grandma had abandoned when going to console Mom.

"Your mother doesn't want you to have any more syrup," Winston said.

My eyebrows shot to my scalp. "But the syrup I

already poured is gone." The standard kid rule of syrup. I pointed in case he needed proof. "See?"

Winston looked at my pancake then looked back at me. "It soaked in. It didn't evaporate. You don't need more."

I turned the bottle upside down and squeezed anyway. Because even if Winston was an adult in a kid's body, he still looked like a kid, which meant he had no authority over me. "I don't *need* more. I *want* more."

Maybe the body swap happened for a reason. Maybe I could help this man-boy learn to have fun once again.

I licked my sticky, sweet fork in hopes of reaching his inner child. "Mm …"

"Snowman pancakes?" Christine trudged out of the bedroom wearing a "World's Best Grandma" T-shirt that hung past her knees.

I grinned. If I didn't know that all Christine's clothes had washed down the river, I would have believed myself to be the only kid in the house who avoided the Freaky Friday mishap. "Yep. With marshmallows and lots of syrup."

Christine scanned the room until her gaze landed on Mom resting on the couch, then smiled a huge smile and raced toward the breakfast bar.

I'd like to see Winston just try to stop her from

drowning her pancake snowman in syrup.

Except Christine didn't climb on the barstool next to me. She raced right past to the mudroom.

I frowned.

Barking?

Oh yeah. Puppies! We hadn't been able to see them last night with all the commotion from the police officers, emergency workers, and the ambulance drive to the hospital. In the light of morning, the whole thing still felt like a dream. But that was no excuse.

I dropped my fork and jumped from my stool. Christine was already opening the kennel when I joined her.

The little fluff balls spilled out onto the linoleum while their mama alternated between licking our hands and blocking us from her babies.

I knelt beside her and rubbed behind her ears as her unblinking, super-blue eyes focused on me. "Hey, Sapphire. Remember us?"

She gave me what might be considered a doggy hug with a paw on my shoulder before focusing back on her pups.

I counted.

Five. Oh, wait. There was another little guy climbing out of the kennel. Six puppies. Except he was half the size of the others.

"Oh, the poor runt." Christine scooped him up.

I played with the remaining puppies, but a huge question popped out of my brain like one of those thought bubbles in comic books. Could Grandma sell a runt puppy? What if nobody wanted it? What if she had to give it away? What if I got to take it home with me? That would be the best Christmas gift ever.

Christine carried the runt out to the living room.

I followed with another puppy, not wanting to appear overeager. How could I make Grandma think that giving me a puppy was all her own idea? "Hey, Grandma?" I sank to the ground, snuggling the little guy under my chin. "The puppy Christine is holding looks smaller than this one."

Grandma turned from Mom on the couch and joined us on the carpet. "He is. Sometimes that happens."

I bit my tongue to keep from screaming out, "Can-I-have-him?" I exhaled slowly to sound calm as I asked, "Will you still sell him?"

Grandma took the pup from Christine to examine him closer for a moment. "I have another week before I can send them to a new home, so we'll see how he's doing by then." She handed the puppy back. "And actually Joey, if you want to help out, I need you to take

23

Sapphire on a walk so that I can give this guy an extra bottle. She doesn't give him enough attention, and if she sees me feeding him, she'll figure she can ignore him completely."

I scrunched my face up and looked toward my mom. Too bad she didn't have the same philosophy as Sapphire. I'd rather have Grandma feed me any day.

Winston stood, rinsed his plate that hadn't had enough syrup on it to even get sticky, and loaded it in the dishwasher. "I'll take her, Grandmother. Joey doesn't have any clothes to wear outside."

I knew where Grandpa kept the sled. If I held Sapphire's leash right, she could pull me along and I wouldn't have to walk at all. "My clothes are in the dryer, I think." I hoped. Though with Mom being injured, I couldn't be sure. "I'll take her."

Grandma pushed to her feet to get Sapphire's leash. "Why don't you boys both take her?"

Would Winston be on board with my sled idea? I shot him a skeptical look.

He beamed. "A brilliant suggestion."

We would see.

I put on my clothes from the dryer—even though they were still slightly damp—and joined Winston in the back yard.

He was wearing a stocking hat. In the shape of Santa's hat but knit in different colored stripes with a yarn pom-pom at the end.

I wouldn't be caught dead in that thing, but I didn't want to hurt the kid's feelings. "Nice hat."

"Thanks. My mother made it."

Aunt Polly. My dad's brother's wife. She and Uncle Alex had gone to Europe for Christmas. At first I'd been excited Winston wasn't going with them, but now I wasn't so sure.

"She actually made you a hat, too." He extended one hand.

I turned and flinched, hoping Mom wouldn't make me wear one of Aunt Polly's crazy creations, but when I finally peeked an eye open, I didn't see a replica of Winston's stocking cap. I saw what looked like a regular knit cap with an attached, fake knit beard and mustache to cover my face. "Cool." I slid the thing over my head.

Winston was an adult disguised as a kid, and I'd be a kid disguised as an adult. Maybe he wasn't that bad after all. I should give him another chance.

"So what do you say we sit on the sled and let Sapphire pull us?"

He chuckled. "I know I haven't seen you for years, but I've heard stories, and that is definitely something I

25

would expect you to do."

I was infamous. Even outside Idaho. How should I respond to such news? "Uh … is that a yes?"

His eyebrows drew together. "Only if I want to break ribs like you do."

I tilted my head. "I haven't broken a rib in almost six months. Come on. You should try it."

"I'm smarter than that."

Oh, now he was questioning my intelligence. I'd show him. "You mean you're boringer?"

"Boringer is not a word. The correct term would be 'more boring.' But no. I am not more boring."

Argh. How was I going to survive two weeks with this guy and his snooty grammar lessons?

I tromped through the snow to the shed to retrieve the wooden sled with the two metal runners.

The thing was probably as old as my dad, but it sure knew how to take a beating. I'd busted through three of our plastic sleds last winter alone.

Maybe my cousin wasn't boring. Just scared. And once I got him out there he'd realize what he'd been missing. "You don't have to be afraid, Winston."

He chuckled that chuckle again. The one that made him sound a little bit like the Joker from Batman.

"What?" I narrowed my eyes at him.

"You're perfect, Joey. Stupidly perfect."

Stupidly perfect? That didn't sound like a good combination. I'd rather be intelligently imperfect. "Why would you say that?"

He knelt down and let Sapphire lick his face. "I asked Grandma about the runt puppy yesterday. She said she might give it to one of us if we can prove ourselves responsible enough to handle him."

I blinked. So that's what all his proper posture, dish-rinsing, dog-walking had been about. He wasn't boring after all. He was conniving. "Grandma will never buy your act." But even as I said the words, my gut churned.

She wouldn't buy such an act from me. No matter how good my intentions, they would never be able to keep me from taking out the sled behind Sapphire. I was in trouble.

Oh, wait! I'd made Grandma that awesome photo frame. Maybe when she saw it, she would see how hard-working and creative I was. "When Grandma sees the present I got her for Christmas, she's going to—"

"The present that washed away with your car?"

My head dropped back toward my shoulder blades. That was right. I had no gift to give Grandma. I had no way to prove my level of responsibility.

I didn't want to walk the dog with Winston anymore.

27

I didn't want him to keep pointing out ways that I was a failure. I yanked Sapphire's leash from his hands and plopped down on the sled.

"You're going to hurt yourself," he said.

"Wanna bet?" The words popped out of my mouth even though I knew better. Even though I'd spent all of last summer learning that betting can ruin the joy of something exciting, like dogsledding.

He shrugged. "Sure."

How did I get myself in these situations? I shifted uncomfortably in my still-damp jeans. I couldn't wait to get the walk over with so I could go back in the cozy house and take them off.

Winston stood there all warm and smug.

I wished he was as cold as I was. "Loser has to take off his clothes and shoes and run in his underwear to the mailbox and back." There. That would teach him. I smiled beneath my scratchy, fake beard and mustache.

He wrinkled his nose. "Why would you want to do that?"

Ha. Like he was going to win. "I don't." I situated myself securely with my heels digging into the front bar of the sled and cracked the leash like the reigns of a harness. "Go, Sapphire!"

Sapphire took off toward the woods and my sled

28

trailed after her smoothly. The best way to walk a dog ever. Winston was so missing out. But he wouldn't be missing out on the jog to the mailbox.

Wind stung what was exposed of my face, and I closed my dry eyes for just a second.

That's all it took not to see the rock coming.

Bam. My body tried to jolt to a stop on the sled, but the leash kept pulling me forward. I soared Superman-style across a blanket of snow. It was kind of fun actually. I mean, how much could it hurt to land in a blanket of snow? I still wasn't going to lose my bet.

Tree coming!

I let go of the leash too late. My face connected with

the trunk. I fell away from the bark, backward, and stared at the gray clouds overhead. Hesitantly, I touched my face to make sure all of my skin hadn't been completely scraped off. My gloved fingers came away red.

And that's when the pounding in my ears began. It joined the symphony of pain in harmony with the stabbing sensation between my eyes.

Winston's freckled face appeared above me. "You lose."

I considered pretending amnesia. Or acting like I had a concussion and was seeing double. But if I was going to have to run to the mailbox in my underwear, I might as well get it over with right away. Before my parents saw my injury and I was forced to lie on the couch all day, next to Mom, with a bag of frozen peas to my forehead. I kicked off my snow boots. "Can I keep my hat on?"

Winston narrowed his eyes as he looked at me. "Yes. I think that's what's stopping the blood."

"What's bleeding?" Sapphire had come around and was trying to lick my face, and I didn't want to get a wound infected with her doggie germs.

"Just your nose."

I slid out of my jacket. "Oh good." A broken nose wouldn't need stitches. But it might ruin my new

30

mustache.

Oh well. Nothing I could do about that now.

I shivered as I unbuttoned my pants. At least I had on my candy cane boxers. Those were kinda cool, right?

"You're wearing holiday boxers?" Winston didn't sound impressed.

"Hush." It took me much longer to run to the mailbox than I had expected, but that was probably because every freezing step reminded me that I was running half-naked through the snow with a pounding headache. At least if I got lost in the trees, my trail of blood would lead me back to safety.

Sapphire ran beside me, seemingly unbothered by the cold in that sweet fur coat of hers.

We reached the mailbox and turned around. I counted down the seconds until I could jump in a hot shower.

The garage door whirred to life and a motor rumbled. Grandma's shiny new SUV backed up toward me.

I left the packed-down snow of the driveway to avoid getting run over.

The deeper snow in the yard reached my knees.

I hopped from one foot to the other. No way were my toes going to fall off from frostbite.

Tires screeched to a stop beside me and the driver's

31

side window rolled down. Grandma stared at me in my boxers, funny hat, and bloody face.

"Hi, Grandma."

"Where are your clothes? What happened to your nose?"

How to explain? "I … uh …"

She pressed her lips together as if she was trying to refrain from smiling. "Never a dull moment with you, is there?"

"Guess not." It would have been nice to blame it on Winston, but the whole thing had been my perfectly stupid idea. I'd offered to bet. I'd come up with the concept of the undies run. Oh what I wouldn't give to put my damp jeans back on.

"Well." She shook her head with a laugh. "As entertaining as this is, you should probably go back in the cabin before your mother sees you and gets even more stressed out."

Oh boy. Not only was I irresponsible, but I was a burden to others. I'd never get that puppy now. "Yes, Grandma."

"I'm headed to the store to buy you guys some new clothes. Just in case you decide to, you know, put something on." She chuckled again and wiped at her eyes. "I'll be back soon."

"Thanks, Grandma."

She rolled up the window and backed away to reveal Winston on the other side of the driveway, leaning forward with his hands to his knees because he was laughing so hard.

He stood and mimicked me. "'Yes, Grandma. Thanks, Grandma.'"

What a little punk. And all the adults thought he was actually a smart, responsible young man. He even had me fooled there for a while.

But what could I do about it? I reached down to the snow and packed a ball big enough to be Frosty's head.

"Yikes." He took off running.

That didn't stop me. I had experience throwing water balloons. I didn't need my snowball launcher to aim and fire.

Direct hit.

He flew forward at least two feet before landing on his stomach.

And that's when something hit me.

Not a snowball, but an idea.

I could still get Grandma a gift. I would just have to rent myself out as a snowball fight professional. Then I could earn enough money to buy her something great. She'd see I was responsible enough to run a business and

33

thoughtful enough to buy presents.

Winston probably hadn't considered giving her a gift.

He was so going down, and I didn't just mean from a snowball to the back.

Chapter Four:
Have Yourself a Merry Little Contest

Grandma and Grandpa drove us kids downtown later that day. By "downtown," they meant the street of small stores that sold furniture made out of logs, candles that looked like logs, and, well, anything else that could be made out of logs. Just in case anyone forgot we were in the mountains and the forest. Between the stores was a slope that led down to the lake—perfect for sledding and for setting up my new business.

Grandma opened the gate on the back of her SUV for me to get the Snowball Fight Professional sign that I'd made out of ... drumroll, please ... a split log. "Are you sure you don't want to walk down to the corner to get hot chocolate with us?"

So tempting. But I knew I'd warm up quickly after getting hired to start snowball fights. I grabbed my sign and snowball launcher. "Thanks, Grandma, but I've got work to do."

Grandpa patted me on the shoulder. "Be fun and have good."

I smiled at my dad's dad in his suspenders and newsboy cap. Even when he mixed up his words he still made more sense than most people. "Great advice, Grandpa."

He took Christine's hand and started off down the sidewalk.

Winston followed, probably hoping to get some kind of badge for helping them cross the street with one of the orange flags used for stopping traffic.

Grandma dug into her old-fashioned coin purse and produced a wrinkled dollar bill. "I'll be your first customer, Joey. When your father gets here with your mother, shoot him a couple times for me."

Grandma was definitely a breath of fresh air. First the sugar, now the money. Gah. It would hurt to turn her down, but I couldn't use her own money to buy her a Christmas gift. That wasn't responsible at all. "Thanks, Grandma, but I can't throw a snowball at Dad right now. He'll be helping Mom with her crutches, and I don't want to cause them both to slip."

Grandma nodded, hopefully considering how

36

The Snowball Fight Professional

responsible I sounded. "You surprise me sometimes, Joey."

Hmm. She'd clearly been less surprised to see me running around outside in my underwear than she was at my choice not to throw a snowball at Dad. Not exactly the impression I'd been going for. "I like to keep my work and play separate."

She downright laughed at that line.

It caught me off guard at first, but then I considered what I did to make money and started laughing, too.

"You know ..." She leaned in as if to whisper conspiratorially. "If you find a way to make money doing something you love, you'll never work a day in your life."

Grandma might possibly have been the cleverest person I'd ever met. "That's why you breed huskies?"

Her gray eyes twinkled. "That's why I breed huskies."

I sighed. I didn't only want one of her huskies; I wanted to be as cool as she was someday. "You're awesome, Grandma."

More laughter. She tucked the dollar back in her coin purse. "I'll stop bothering you so you can get

Angela Ruth Song

to work, kiddo. Might even use this money to bring you back some hot chocolate."

"Sweet." I referred to her as well as the beverage and my job. Everything about the Christmas season was sweet.

"Josiah Michaels?" A girl wearing a pink camo jacket and carrying a sled that looked more like a snowboard trudged my way up the hill.

"Isabelle Lancaster." Did I say that everything about the Christmas season was sweet? I had spoken too soon—my neighbor girl was apparently in McCall for the holidays.

I actually had a crush on Isabelle at one time. We even ran a business together for a while, but we could never agree on how to split the tasks. Mom said she was too much like me.

"What happened to your nose?" She wrinkled up hers.

"I got run over by a reindeer." I might as well have been run over what with the way Mom freaked out about my little collision. Apparently, girls thought it was a big deal when part of a guy's face turned black and blue. But Dad had talked Mom out of making another trip to the emergency room. Paying a doctor to examine a male, middle-school

38

brain could waste too much of his money. And waste my valuable snowball-fighting time.

"Very funny. What's that?" She pointed at my snowball launcher.

"Nothing." I turned my back to her and set up my Snowball Fight Professional sign against a bronze statue of bears on a wall.

She leaned up against the bears like she was Goldilocks or something. "I know what you're doing."

"I hope so," I said. "Otherwise you might have to go back to elementary school so you can learn how to read."

She flipped her hair over her shoulder. "How much are you charging for the snowball launcher?"

I knelt down to start stacking snowballs. I needed to be ready for all the business that would soon come my way. "Just a quarter to start out."

I couldn't charge the same amount as I had for a water balloon in the summer because water balloons were rarer. Anybody could bend over and make himself a snowball. That's where the launcher came in. Hopefully kids wanted me to use the launcher since it could shoot farther than they could throw.

39

"If I pay you a quarter, could I shoot the launcher?"

"Oh no. I'm not letting you try to take over another one of my businesses."

She lifted her snowboard sled. "How about a trade?"

I wrapped my arms around my snowball launcher. How would the poor guy feel if I traded him first chance I got? It may be an appealing offer, but I could never let my launcher know I was considering the idea. "Not happening."

Her lips stuck out in a pout.

I went back to my snowball forming and ignored her. I'd seen that trick before. I had a sister, remember? Just because girls acted all cute didn't mean they should get their way.

"Are you going to shoot a couple snowballs to draw attention to your business?"

I hadn't thought that far ahead, but I wasn't going to let her know that. "Yes."

"Do you want to shoot them at me?"

I narrowed my eyes. There was nobody I'd rather shoot more, but no girl went from a pouty lip to offering to get a fat lip without there being a catch. "What's the catch?"

40

She shrugged. "I just thought we could take turns riding down the hill on my snowboard sled and shooting at each other."

I pointed a gloved finger at her. "Aha."

She blinked in innocence. "I'm trying to help you out."

Whatever. "I'm not buying it. Now go away. I've got work to do."

"Fine." Her overly sweet tone went with her overly sweet smile. "I'll just go ride down the hill while you shoot your snowballs at nobody."

She sashayed away.

Finally. Now I could shoot my snowballs … at nobody.

How about the bear statues? But they were too close a target to really impress people. So I aimed at the trees.

A few kids watched for a bit but went back to their sledding without hiring me.

I huffed and the cloud of my breath slowly floated away. I sure could have used that hot cocoa Grandma had offered.

Without turning my neck, I slid my eyes sideways as Isabelle glided down the hill standing up, kind of like she was snowboarding.

I loved snowboarding, but with Mom laid up, we might not get to go this year. Maybe I could ask for a snowboard sled for Christmas. Or maybe I could borrow Isabelle's. No. I wasn't going to give in to her that easily.

Though, she was a moving target.

I lifted the barrel of my blaster and followed her progress down the hill. Knocking her off the sled would definitely get the attention I wanted. So far nobody had even asked how much it would cost for me to shoot the launcher for them.

But, no. I was going to stick to my guns.

I grimaced and looked at the only gun I'd brought. "What do you think, boy? Are you willing to let Isabelle shoot you so we can see a little action here?"

I shook the snowball launcher up and down as if it were nodding.

Who was I to argue with my new toy? I lifted the blaster to my shoulder again and focused on Isabelle in the distance.

She was almost to the bottom of the hill. I'd have to act fast.

Bam. Bam. Bam. I pulled the trigger three times in a row.

Isabelle went flying. Head over feet. The snowboard sled sailed one way and she sailed another, landing face first in a snowbank by the dock. Her face reappeared. Except for the toothy grin, her whole head was covered in snow.

Awesome.

She wiped her face, grabbed her board, and charged up the hill toward me. "My turn."

I sighed like I was doing her a big favor, but honestly, I couldn't get my feet in the straps of her board fast enough. "Good luck hitting me."

She lifted the weapon.

I pushed off before she could fire. A close range blow would probably feel more like a paintball-gun attack.

The angle of the hill whisked me away.

I pressed my feet into the board and pulled my belly tight to keep balanced. I shifted this way and that to avoid little kids on toboggans. The wind stung, but in a good way. In a way that made me so glad I'd agreed to Isabelle's offer. Even if she didn't hit me and bring in business, I still got a great thrill ride. Maybe next time I'd build a little ramp to jump off. Because this was way too easy. I was already halfway down the hill.

43

Oof!

Was that a rock that hit me in the back? I wobbled but stayed upright.

Pftt … The second snowball whizzed past my head.

"You missed me, you missed me, now you gotta … never mind." Kissing her hadn't worked out all that well last time. I looked over my shoulder to make sure she hadn't heard my silly chant. *Oof.* Right in the kisser. But I couldn't consider the irony of that as I was too busy flying backwards off the board and tumbling down the hill. If I picked up any more speed, my whole body would turn into a giant snowball.

The good news was that the hill ended. The bad news was that it ended where the lake began, and I skidded out across the frozen water.

The ice gets pretty thick in the winter—thick enough even to ride snowmobiles on. But with my recent river experience, I wasn't willing to risk it. I scrambled back to shore and made the trek up the hill to find kids lining up to pay Isabelle to shoot *my* launcher. "Hey!"

She flashed me one of her angelic smiles, then blasted a snowball past me to knock over a teenager.

44

The kids cheered, and the one closest to her handed over a wad of cash. Really?

I extended my palm for the snowball launcher. She better not argue.

She laid my baby in my hands then started splitting up the money. As if I was going to share it with her.

"My gun, my income."

Kids started to disperse since no more snowballs were being fired.

"Wait, guys," I called. "I'll shoot the snowballs for you."

The last kid in the crowd stuck his tongue at me and jumped on a snow disc. Nice.

Isabelle smirked before handing over the moolah. "You can have it all, Joe. But if you are the owner of this business, then you'll have to pay me as an employee to shoot at me again."

I pointed to the snowboard sled. "I thought we had a deal."

"We did."

"And?" I shook my head and frowned. I was usually the one in control. But somehow she had me almost begging her to work.

"*And* I'm renegotiating."

Angela Ruth Strong

Of course she was. "That's cold."

She rubbed her arms and shivered. "No. I'm going to keep warm by sledding. You're the one who'll be left out in the cold."

I rolled my eyes. That would have been the end of that, except the eye roll landed on the bills in my hand.

Four bucks? Four bucks! In the little amount of time it took me to hike up the hill. With this kind of money, I could buy Grandma something super fantastic.

My mind reeled with the possibilities of things Grandma liked.

Baking—I could buy her an apron. No. Too girly. If anybody gave Grandma an apron it should be Christine.

Dogs—I could buy her a remote control treat dispenser for Sapphire. No. Too robotic. Grandma was kind of old school.

Living in cabins—I could buy her a snowmobile to make it easier for her to check her mail every day. No. If I made enough money to buy a snowmobile, then I could probably afford to buy the puppy myself.

Which was a fun idea.

46

"Wait."

Isabelle looked over her shoulder. "Yes?"

Hands fisted, I squeezed my eyes shut. I didn't want to say the words. I didn't want to hand over the money.

But if I really wanted a puppy, I had to.

"I will hire you for a dollar a run."

One corner of her lips curled up. "One dollar every time I sled down the hill and let you shoot me?"

My stomach churned. If shooting her didn't bring in big bucks, then the money she'd already made me would dwindle fast. Better do a couple trial runs to see how well the plan worked. "I'll only hire you for two runs to start off with. After that, we'll renegotiate. Again."

Now both sides of her mouth curled up. "You know if you make good money, I'm going to ask for a raise, right?"

I swallowed hard. I didn't want to pay Isabelle a higher wage, but I also didn't want to have to keep paying her every time she sledded down the hill if it didn't help my business. Sometimes a business man had to take a risk if he wanted money to buy his grandmother a present so she would give him a

47

puppy. "I know."

"Deal." My very first employee strapped on her sled and took off down the hill.

She'd be taking my earnings with her if I didn't get busy. I loaded my snowball launcher, aimed, and fired. And yeah, I laughed a little as she flew backwards into a snowbank. That was worth a dollar even if it didn't bring in business.

But it did. Seven kids lined up to have me blast their friends off sleds with two snowballs apiece before Isabelle made it back up the hill. All right, I missed one target, so I didn't end up charging the client. But that still added up to three dollars. I handed Isabelle her earnings.

She eyed my money. "I'm glad you didn't lock in my rate."

I stuffed the rest of the cash in my pocket. Maybe after this run I'd hire somebody else to help me. Somebody not as business savvy. But I'd worry about that later. For now I had to concentrate on knocking her off the snowboard sled.

She strapped her feet in and pushed away.

I loaded three more snowballs and peered down the muzzle of the best snowball launcher ever.

Three seconds and she'd be right in front of a group of teenagers.

If I hit her at that spot, they'd be sure to notice and want to hire me to get involved in the action.

Three, two, one, fi—

A freight train rammed into my back. Well, maybe not a freight train, but it sure felt like one. I couldn't even take a step to find my balance before whatever it was that rammed into me knocked me face first into the snow. I pushed my hands against the snow to stand up but a weight on my back held me down.

Had some kid flown off his sled and landed on me?

Familiar laughter. Either it was the villain from my favorite superhero movie on my back or my cousin was the culprit.

Chapter Five:
Do You Fear What I Fear?

I lifted my head out of the stinging snow and blinked a couple times to get the melting flakes out of my eyes before cranking my neck to confront Winston. "Get off me, you punk."

Winston didn't move. "I'm the punk?"

Duh. "You're the one who tackled me."

"You are the one who was going to shoot snowballs at a girl."

You've got to be kidding me. Winston wanted to protect my neighbor? She was so much tougher than he would ever be. "I wasn't shooting snowballs at a girl. I was shooting them at Isabelle."

"Joey, I'm disappointed in you. First you try to hurt her, then you disrespect her?"

I could lie there on the ground with him on me while trying to explain the whole story, or I could give him the quick version and push him off if he didn't move. "She wanted me to shoot her."

51

He clicked his tongue. "You expect me to believe that?"

Story time was over. I'd claw my way out from under him like one of those bears in the statue. I dug my fingers into the snow, arched my back, and rumbled the start of a growl.

Isabelle charged up the hill. "Joe, you missed me." She stopped and stared at Winston on my back.

I grunted. "I got tackled."

Winston picked this time to let me go. He stood properly as if he were Prince Charming climbing off his noble steed.

I didn't feel so noble, though. In fact, I wished I'd skipped the explanation altogether and thrown him to the ground before Isabelle had reappeared.

"Are you all right?" Winston asked as if she were a damsel in distress.

Her head tilted to one side, and she dropped her sled.

If I didn't know what it looked like to have chapped skin from the wind, I'd think she was even blushing.

"I'm fine." But it didn't sound like the way she would normally say it. In fact, it sounded more like Christine-with-a-crush.

I pushed to a kneeling position and shook my head. Maybe I'd hit it harder than I realized because I had to be imagining Isabelle's reaction to my cousin.

"Oh good." Winston reached out and patted her arm. "I was worried when I saw Joey aim his snowball bazooka at you."

Bazooka? I liked the sound of it. And Isabelle would, too. I waited for her to tell him that she was my employee and back up my story.

"You ... you tackled Joe to rescue me?"

"Of course I tackled him to rescue you. I don't go around tackling just anybody for no reason."

She giggled.

I dropped back on my rump and stared at Isabelle and Winston standing above me. This wasn't the Isabelle I knew. The Isabelle I knew would see right through a devious little punk like him. And even if he had truly wanted to rescue her, she didn't need rescuing in the first place.

Enough was enough.

I jumped up and held out a dollar bill. "Here you go, Isabelle. I guess I will pay you even though my cousin here interfered in our business arrangement." Hopefully my gesture would show her that I was the bigger man, as well as put an end to Winston's knight-in-shining-armor act.

Winston frowned at the money. "What's that for?"

Angela Ruth Song

"Oh." Isabelle shrugged, still not looking at me. "Joe hired me. I let him knock me off my snowboard sled so he can attract attention to his snowball business."

"What?" Winston's eyes widened in mock shock. "That's dangerous. You could bruise or scrape your pretty face."

Her eyelashes lowered and brushed against pink cheeks.

Was she seriously buying this bologna? I thought Winston's performance would only work on grandparents. She needed to snap out of it. "Isabelle, it's time to renegotiate your contract. How about—"

"How about I get you some hot chocolate?" Winston held his elbow out for her to take and then turned her away from me. "You don't need Joey's money when I'm here to take care of you."

She actually let him push her forward a couple steps. The girl who could—and should!—pulverize Winston just turned to mush instead.

I stood frozen to my spot, and not only because it was cold outside.

"I'll be there in a second," Winston called ahead to Isabelle before winking at me. "You don't have a thing for her, do you, cousin?"

A thing? "No." Absolutely not. That wasn't why I felt

54

like I'd just been impaled by an icicle.

"So you were only using her to help you earn enough money to buy Grandma a gift and get her to give you the runt puppy?"

How does the kid know these things? "Uh …"

"Don't waste your time. I'm already making more than you with my snow-shoveling business, *and* I know what Grandma wants for Christmas."

Oh, pooper scooper. I still hadn't even planned what I was going to buy once I made enough money to go shopping. Winston was way ahead of me.

He swiped the dollar bill from my hand. "I'll make sure your friend gets this. She'd rather hang out with me anyway. What's her name again?"

I stared at my hard-earned money. Should I fight for it? If anybody saw us fighting, they'd blame me and not Winston. I'd be the one to get in trouble. Not the kid who dressed fancy and shoveled snow and rescued girls from hooligans with snowball bazookas.

I didn't answer, but the two of them strolled down the street like I didn't even exist anyway.

So what did it matter? I'd already been planning to hire someone else, right?

The thought didn't keep me from scowling at Winston's back. It was one thing to fire an employee. It was another thing to have her quit. Really, though, she hadn't quit, had she? She'd been stolen.

What could she possibly see in Winston? She'd figure out how boring he was soon enough. And hopefully I'd be around to watch her dump whatever drink he bought her on top of his silly hat.

For now, I had to get back to work. Winston thought he'd won, but while he was off making goo-goo eyes at Isabelle, I'd have my chance to earn more money than him. Maybe this Isabelle thing could work out after all.

"Can I shoot your snowball blaster?"

I turned to find a boy about Christine's age staring up at me with wide, brown eyes. I'd planned to have kids pay for *me* to shoot the blaster, but now that that market disappeared with Isabelle, maybe I would make more money if I rented it out. "Fifty cents."

"Oh." The kid hung his head, showing the top of thick, shaggy hair.

Poor kid. Didn't even have a hat for his head. Must not have two quarters either.

"Hey, how about I pay you to let me shoot you? You can be my employee and make some extra money for Christmas." I would have preferred to hire an older kid, but since this boy had shown the most interest in my weapon, he would probably be the best choice.

He looked back up. "Really?"

Finally. Somebody who would let me be the boss. "Sure. It will help me bring in business."

"Okay. What do I do?"

Isabelle had left her snowboard sled behind, so we could use that, but first we'd have to make more ammunition. I dropped to my knees. "Help me pack snowballs."

The kid knelt down in his jeans. Where were his snow pants? He'd be soaked in no time, and I knew from my undies run that morning how miserable wet pants could be.

"You don't have to kneel," I said. "I'll just hand you the snowballs and you can put them in a pile." I packed. I handed him a ball.

It slipped out of his fingers and splatted on the ground.

I frowned at his oversized gloves. No wonder he couldn't hold onto anything. "Your gloves are too big. Don't you have some smaller ones?"

He pulled at the gloves as if to make them fit tighter. "These are fine. They have growing room."

Growing room? That was a term Mom and Dad fought over when buying me sneakers. Dad always wanted my shoes to have "growing room" so that I didn't grow out of them as fast. It was a money-saving thing. The kid must have a dad like mine. "Oh. Well, just hold onto the snowballs real tight then."

"Okay."

We assembled our ammo in silence, though my mind was busy. If this kid helped me out and we worked the business the way Isabelle and I had been doing, then I could make a couple bucks with every one of his sled runs. That could add up rather quickly.

How much money had Winston made with his snow shoveling? If it was anything like my friend Chance's lawn-mowing business, he probably made about ten bucks an hour. I could easily make more than that. Then I'd just have to find out what it was he was going to buy Grandma for Christmas and buy it first.

"Joe!"

Dad? I looked up to find my father yelling at me from Grandpa's old pickup truck.

I waved.

Dad motioned me over.

Bad timing. But I'd better go see what he wanted. "I'll be right back," I told my new employee.

He nodded, so I ran over to the truck.

Mom sat in the passenger seat with her head back and eyes squeezed shut. At least I thought it was my mom.

58

I'd never seen her so still.

"Mom is feeling queasy from her pain meds, so I'm just going to take her home. You can stay and come home with Grandma and Grandpa, but I need you to help me find Winston first. He wanted to go back to the cabin early so he could shovel the walk. He's such a responsible kid. Have you seen him?"

Unfortunately. But I didn't say this aloud. Dad wouldn't understand the feelings I had about his dear, sweet, marvelous nephew running off with my previous employee.

Hey, if Winston could sabotage my business, maybe I could sabotage his. If he didn't make the money he was bragging about, then he wouldn't be able to buy Grandma whatever gift he had in mind. This was way too easy.

"I'll shovel the walk."

Dad's eyebrows shot toward the blue and orange Boise State hat Aunt Polly had made for him. "You want to shovel snow?"

Mom's eyes even peeked open for a moment.

I shrugged as if I volunteered for chores all the time. "Sure."

Dad felt my forehead. "Are you okay? Maybe I *should* have taken you to the hospital after you ran into the

59

tree."

I gave what I hoped sounded like a mature chuckle. "Come on, Dad. Grandma and Grandpa do so much for us. I just want to help them out." Help them out of believing Winston's show of being a perfect grandkid.

Dad looked over at Mom who had her eyes closed again. He sighed. "That's really nice of you, Joe. I just wish I wasn't suspicious of your motives."

I wasn't going to respond to that because I didn't want to admit Dad had reason to be suspicious. So I just tilted my head like a hurt puppy.

Dad laughed. "All right. I'll chalk it up to the Christmas spirit. Get in so we can get your mother to bed."

Yes. Winston could drink cocoa with Isabelle all he wanted. In the end, I'd be the one taking home the trophy … er, the puppy. "Let me grab my launcher." I ran back toward the bear statue on the hill. It sat next to a bunch of snowballs the hatless wonder had piled for me. It almost made me wish I hadn't volunteered to shovel the walk.

Almost.

"That's awesome," I said, picking up my launcher. "But I have to go back to my grandparents' house now."

The kid looked up at me with eyes so lonely they

could have been mine last summer when my friends all deserted me to play baseball.

I didn't want him to feel like that. "Will you be here tomorrow?"

His head bobbed up and down.

"Great." Maybe after a day of shoveling and a couple good days of snowball fighting, I'd have enough to buy Grandma a super-sweet Christmas gift.

Gifts. Money.

Oh, I'd better pay the kid for all those snowballs he'd made, just to ensure he'd return to work. I took a glove off to reach into my pocket and pull out a dollar bill. That only left me with four dollars for the day. But at least I'd get paid for shoveling the walk later. "Here you go."

The kid's eyes, somehow, got bigger. "Thank you." He took the money as if it had a picture of Benjamin Franklin on it rather than George Washington.

He must be new to the business world. I'd have to show him the ropes. I held out a hand to shake.

He looked at it as if I was trying to get him to give me the dollar back.

"I'm Joey Michaels," I said, hoping he'd figure out the gesture and the moment wouldn't get any more awkward. "What's your name?"

61

"Oh." His face relaxed and he stuffed the cash in his pocket so he could shake my hand. "My name is Micah."

The oversized glove fell into the snow, which was okay because it allowed for a firm grip when we shook—an important business basic.

"I'll see you tomorrow, Micah."

He pulled his dollar bill back out and probably didn't even notice when I took off.

Christine was already in the back of the truck. Oh no. Did she want to get in on my snow shoveling?

"What are you doing here?" I tried not to sound completely repulsed by her presence. Sometimes little sisters were oversensitive to things like that.

But she just smiled at me and curled into a ball in the corner of the backseat of the truck. "I want to go home to play with the puppies some more."

The warning sirens going off in my head fell silent. Crisis averted.

"Cool."

And life was cool. Or should I say "cold." Like fingers-freezing-in-place-around-the-handle-of-the-snow-shovel cold. Which I found out when we got home and I started clearing the walk.

What was I thinking to volunteer to shovel outside? I must have really hit my head too hard that morning.

The Snowball Fight Professional

"Joey, honey," Grandma called out the front door. She'd returned from town a while ago and the sun had already set, but still I was working on the front steps.

At least, I thought it was Grandma at the door from the silhouette of her body in the light pouring out of the house.

Winston didn't even seem to mind that I'd stolen his job. He kept waving at me out the window and looking at an imaginary watch on his wrist.

What was it Grandma had said about finding a way to make money doing something I loved? I'd certainly failed that one. Though could anybody possibly love shoveling snow?

"How about you come in now that it's dark out?"

A good idea, as sometimes hungry bears woke up early from hibernation in the surrounding woods, and it probably wouldn't be safe for me to be working alone outside all night. Which was how long this job would take me.

"Okay," I said, vowing to never pick up another snow shovel in my life. If that meant moving to Hawaii as soon as I turned eighteen, so be it. I could live with my old mailman, Parker.

"Since you worked so hard today, I'll have Winston shovel the back walk tomorrow. Give you a break."

"No." There went my brilliant idea of stealing Winston's business.

Grandma laughed. "Honey, by the time you finish the back walkway, it will be time to shovel the front again. Winston is really fast at this, and he was planning to do it anyway."

I looked over Grandma's shoulder to find Winston smiling smugly. Of course he was good at shoveling. He was good at everything he did—everything except being the good person he pretended he was.

"Fine." How could I argue? Grandma was right about the time it would take me to shovel. The only thing I could do was hope the back walkway had as much ice on it as this front walkway had.

I stomped my boots to get off the snow before entering the house. And then I stopped and stared at the snow falling off my boots and melting on the wood floor inside the cabin.

There *was* something else I could do other than simply wish Winston a bunch of ice. I could make sure the back walkway was icy.

That would keep him shoveling all day. He wouldn't be as fast as Grandma thought he was. He might not even be as fast as I'd been in the front. Thus, he wouldn't have time to shovel anybody else's walkway. He'd be stuck doing the one job while I was making a financial killing with my snowballs down by the lake.

I stepped backward out the front door.

"Where are you going, honey?" asked Grandma.

"Uh …" I couldn't let them know what I had planned. "I forgot something." Really, I had. I'd forgotten to come up with this plan before entering the cabin.

"Oh?" She peered past me into the night. Actually we hadn't even had dinner yet, but it sure looked like night out there. "Well, don't be long. I just pulled my pecan pie cookies out of the oven."

I sniffed. Sugar and spice and everything nice. That's what grandmas were made of. I gave her a huge grin. "Give me two seconds." I tromped through the snow around the back of the cabin and dug the hose out of the shed where I'd seen it stored next to the sled. Bingo.

Bingo? That would be a good name for the puppy I was sure to get in my stocking now.

After attaching the hose to the outdoor spigot, I pointed the nozzle toward the back walkway and pulled the trigger.

It sputtered and squealed twice before a nice, long stream of water rained down on the snowy cement. Soon the sidewalk would turn into an ice-skating rink.

Winston would have a fine time plowing that up in the morning.

Dad's shadow appeared in the window above me. I jumped. But he hadn't seen me. He was just sneaking the first cookie.

I sighed in relief and twisted the faucet, turning the water off. It took me a little longer to roll the hose back up, but I still beat everybody else in racing Dad to the second batch of cookies.

We smiled in mutual satisfaction when biting into the warm, crispy, goodness of Grandma's masterpieces.

"I'm proud of you today, Joe," said Dad.

I shoved the rest of the cookie into my mouth so I didn't have to respond.

"You gave up sledding to shovel the walkway for Grandma and Grandpa. Most kids wouldn't do that, you know."

I turned my back to grab the milk from the fridge. I couldn't look Dad in the eye. I thought I'd done something pretty great today, but it was not the same thing Dad thought I'd done. And I didn't want him to be disappointed in me. Again.

Chapter Six:
It's Beginning to Look a Lot Like Christmas Shopping

Cinnamon rolls in the shape of a Christmas wreath for breakfast? I loved waking up at the cabin.

Willie Wonka had nothing on Grandma.

"Mm…" I licked my sugary fingers and shot my napkin toward the garbage can as if I were shooting a free throw. "And it's good." That was the only kind of free throw I could make, actually.

Grandpa hobbled over to the waste basket and pulled out the almost-full bag. "Joey, would you get another liner?" he asked.

"Sure, Grandpa." I hopped from the barstool and sock-slid to the pantry.

Dad beamed as if he truly thought I was becoming this kid who enjoyed doing chores. Probably hoped to put "lines garbage cans" on my résumé and send me out to seek my first real job.

But the truth was that I liked getting trash liners out of the pantry because it gave me the chance to swipe candy canes. If Dad was still thinking about my snow shoveling last night …

Oh no. Last night. The back sidewalk.

I stuck my head out of the pantry to make sure Grandpa wasn't taking the garbage out the back way.

The back door slammed shut with a bang. No Grandpa in sight. Since when did he start hobbling so fast?

I sock-slid to the door and yanked it open.

Whew. He hadn't made it down the steps.

"I'll take that out, Grandpa."

Grandpa waved me away. "You just take care of the liner, Joey. I will take this out because I have to unhook the bear on the garbage can that keeps the straps out."

I pushed away the mental image of a bear hooked to a trash can because Grandpa meant to say that he had to unhook the strap that kept the bears out, and I planned to give him a hard time about it, but not until he was safely back in the house. "Wait!" I leaped in front of him, ignoring the cold sting of ice coming through my socks.

Grandpa looked down at my stocking feet. "Your grandmother told me you were running around out here in your underwear yesterday. I'm having none of that. Go back inside until you put on shoes and a coat."

"But—"

"Now." He was a bossy old guy when he wanted to be.

I raced back in the door to grab my jacket and boots, checking over my shoulder to make sure I could still see his head through the window.

Maybe he wouldn't slip after all. Maybe the flakes that fell during the night created enough texture on the ice to keep it from being slippery. Maybe—

"Whoa!" Grandpa's arms flailed in the air.

Trash burst from the garbage bag, spreading over the snow.

I dropped my second boot and charged like a bull

69

toward the back door.

But Winston's pounding feet beat me to it. And he was the one to leap out just in time and catch Grandpa as his legs slipped out from underneath him.

The back door slammed in my face. I stared through the window at the suddenly peaceful scene before me with Grandpa sitting in Winston's lap in a snowbank littered with napkins, an orange juice carton, egg shells, and a ripped-up garbage bag.

The rest of my family crowded behind me.

I wasn't sure whether to go down the steps to help Grandpa, acting as surprised as everybody else was at the catastrophe, or to run to the bathroom and puke. I wouldn't even have to fake sick.

Dad pulled open the door. "What happened?"

"I think I slipped," said Grandpa, looking around as if unsure of where he was.

If only he hadn't been so adamant about unhooking those bears from the garbage can.

"Are you okay?" Christine pushed around me, carrying the littlest husky with her onto the back porch.

Mom followed on crutches.

Then Grandma with a tissue to her eyes.

I hung back—afraid that Grandpa wasn't going to be able to get up. Afraid that maybe when he said, "I think

70

I slipped," what he meant was "I think I slipped a disk in my back."

I wanted to say I was sorry, but even more I wanted them not to know this was my fault.

Mom's crutch slid sideways. She grabbed onto the porch railing while Dad jumped down the stairs to help Grandpa up.

I gritted my teeth. What if Dad's feet slid out from underneath him as well?

He landed safely before hoisting Grandpa to a standing position.

Grandma stayed on the porch with Mom, testing the surface of the ground with the toe of her orthotic shoe. "This is really slick today."

Christine squatted down and set the little husky on the ice.

Its paws immediately shot out four different directions so that it landed on its belly.

She giggled. "The puppy can't even walk."

"That's so strange," said Grandma. "We put salt out here the other day to melt the ice.

I covered my face like I was a toddler again and believed that if I couldn't see people, then they couldn't see me. But I still wanted to know what was going on, so I peeked through my fingers anyway.

Winston grinned at me.

If ever there was a need for Grandpa's duct tape, it was over Winston's mouth. But I doubted that would have stopped him from ratting me out. He would have mimed, in great detail, my role in the hazardous environment.

"I'm so glad I was fast enough to catch you, Grandfather." Winston replaced his smile with a look of alarm.

Of course, that smile would have been only for me. Everyone else was supposed to see him as the self-sacrificial hero. And they did.

"You're quick," said Dad.

"You're strong," said Mom.

"What would we have done without you, Winston?" asked Grandma.

"Thank you, my boy," said Grandpa.

"It was nothing." Winston deserved an Academy Award for the way he waved off the praise. "I'm just curious as to how this ground got so slick." He knelt down and tapped on the shiny sheet of ice. "It's almost as if somebody hosed it down last night."

Christine narrowed her eyes.

Pooper scooper. It was only a matter of time now.

"Who would do that?" asked Grandma.

"I don't know." Winston stroked his chin as if he were wearing the beard that came with my hat. "Who was out here last night?"

"Only Joey," said Grandma. "But why would he do such a thing?"

All heads turned my direction.

My stomach lurched, which made it really hard to focus on racking my brain for some rational excuse as to why I iced down the back walkway. Nothing came to mind. Absolutely nothing.

"Joey?" asked Mom. "Did you do this?"

I opened my mouth but didn't get a chance to respond before Winston was tracking down more clues.

"And over here"—he might as well have announced "Exhibit B" in the case against me as he walked toward the spigot—"someone has clearly used the garden hose recently."

Grandma gasped.

"Why?" Grandpa demanded.

"What if *I* had slipped?" asked Mom. "I could have injured my good ankle."

Oh boy. I hadn't thought of that.

"Joe?" Dad prompted, hands on hips. He didn't have to say it, but his eyes told me that he'd never been more disappointed.

73

I couldn't defend myself from this one. I hung my head. "It was a prank. I thought it would be funny for Winston to have to shovel as long as I did. I didn't think anybody would get hurt."

Mom grasped her chest as if I'd given her a heart attack. At least she was back to her old dramatic self.

"You're grounded from sledding today, young man," said Dad.

Everybody else filed back into the house to let him lecture me in private. Everybody but Winston, who'd offered to pick up all the garbage on the ground. It made it very hard to listen to Dad when I knew Perfect Winston was eavesdropping on the whole conversation and taking pleasure in my pain.

But it really didn't matter what lesson Dad was trying to teach me. I'd already learned it. The hard way.

He ended with his typical, "Do you understand me, son?"

"Yes."

"Then look me in the eye."

I glanced up and tried to focus, but there in the background was Winston with his arms crossed and chin in the air. If Dad hadn't been in hearing range, he probably would have been chanting, "Neener-neener-neener."

"So I'm taking your snowball launcher away for—"

"What?" Dad said he was taking away my baby?

Dad held up a hand to hush me. "I'm taking it away for the day. If you can prove yourself responsible by going shopping with your mother and carrying around her packages, then I will consider giving it back to you tomorrow."

"Shopping?" Was my snowball launcher worth a day of shopping? My eyes slid toward Winston. Yes. I would do anything to get my weapon back. The punk wouldn't get away with this.

"Yes, shopping." Dad cleared his throat, probably questioning if his punishment was too severe. But punishing me meant freedom for him. He'd get to go watch Boise State play the University of Idaho in the "black and blue" rivalry hockey game at Manchester Ice Rink while I followed Mom around the cluttered stores that smelled like soap. "And if Mom tells me you whined or complained at all, it will be at least another day until you get your toy back."

"It's not a toy."

"Joe." The warning voice.

"Yes, sir."

"You also need to write your grandparents an apology letter before you leave. And return any money

75

my mom paid you for shoveling."

That was even worse than shopping. It was the opposite of shopping. It meant I wouldn't be able to shop for Grandma. It also meant admitting that I could have seriously hurt Grandpa. And I didn't want to think about that.

I nodded and trudged inside to write the letter. Maybe if I ever did make any money, I could offer to get Grandpa one of those buttons to wear around his neck so he could automatically call an ambulance when he fell. Maybe anybody who hung around me should have one of those.

Christine joined me at the desk in Grandpa's office, petting a puppy. "Hey," she whispered. And not a look-what-I've-got-and-you-don't whisper.

So I turned toward her instead of ignoring her like I normally did. "What?"

She glanced over her shoulder. "I think Winston knew you sprayed the hose."

Everybody knew now. "Yeah, he figured it out."

"No, I mean I think he knew it was slick out there and that Grandpa would fall."

I scratched my head. "How would he know?"

She shrugged. "I don't know, but when Grandpa pulled the trash liner out of the trash can, Winston put his shoes on and moved toward the door."

I rubbed my face. "But that would mean Winston wanted Grandpa to fall to make me look bad." He couldn't be that evil. I mean, he liked it when I failed, but he hadn't set me up to fail, had he?

She nodded, eyes unblinking.

"Oh man."

It was like when we were little kids and Winston would kick me when nobody was looking. Then, if I kicked back, he would cry to Mom and I would have to go to the "penalty box," as Dad called it. Except now we were old enough to know better.

Ha. Here I'd thought he was a man in a kid's body, but really he was as immature as a toddler.

"Why doesn't he like you?" Christine asked.

There were lots of reasons people didn't like me. Girls when I ignored them, or jocks when I got stuck on their sports team in P.E. and ruined their chance of winning, or adults who thought I caused trouble. But why would my own cousin not like me?

Christine shifted her weight to catch the wiggly little husky as it squirmed out of her grip.

That was it. "He wants the puppy."

Christine held the fluff ball next to her face. "Who wouldn't?"

"No. I mean Grandma told him that if one of us was responsible enough to take care of a dog, she might give the runt to us. So he's acting all responsible and trying to make me look bad." Yeah, yeah, I've been doing the same thing. But he was the one getting away with it.

"You really thought you were in the running?" asked Christine.

I wrinkled my sore nose at her. Ouch.

She nudged my shoulder. "I didn't mean it that way. It's a serious question. You haven't been acting very responsible at all. I mean, you were outside in your underwear yesterday."

Was I ever going to live that one down? "I have a plan to show my responsibility," I muttered. Not that it mattered now.

"What is it?"

I sighed. Once I said it out loud, it would sound really stupid. "I was going to make money with a snowball business and buy Grandma a really nice gift."

"Ohh …" Her voice was a whisper of awe. "That's brilliant."

"Really?" I'd never imagined Christine would ever refer to any of my ideas as brilliant. Unfortunately she was wrong in this instance. "I mean *not* really. Winston makes more money than I do. Plus, he knows what

Grandma wants."

Christine smooshed her lips together in thought. "You could get her an apron."

I wasn't going to tell my sister what a dumb idea that was right after she'd referred to me as brilliant for the first time. "Maybe."

"I know." She leaned in. "I'll stay home with Grandma today and see if she will tell me what she wants, then I'll call you when I find out. If you're really good for Mom today, I bet she'll loan you the money to buy the gift."

"Hmm …" Could I do it? Could I tell Christine how excellent I thought her plan was? Nope. "Why are you helping me?"

"You don't know?" She snuggled the puppy up to her cheek.

Now it all made sense. "You want Grandma to give me the puppy so you can play with it at home."

"Yes," she said in her pouty baby voice that usually drove me crazy. She held the puppy up to my face so that its fur tickled my nose.

I couldn't keep from laughing. "All right. I'm in."

I'd have to be really extra good when shopping with Mom. There was a first for everything, right?

Chapter Seven:
What Child Did This?

"Isn't this adorable, Joey?"

I trudged after Mom through The Christmas House. Could I get away with saying, "Yes, it's adorable," without actually looking at the 98th thing she'd called adorable over the past two hours? But being that I was supposed to be on my best behavior, I turned to look.

A leather journal with a pine cone clasp.

Oh no. If I agreed with her that it was adorable, would she put it in my stocking? Then would she force me to write in it every day? Shopping with Mom was even more dangerous than walking on an icy sidewalk.

I needed a quick diversion. I grabbed a box in front of me. "I think this is adorable," I said before I even knew what I held in my hand.

Whew. Ninjabread cookie cutters. That *was* pretty adorable.

Mom tilted her head in disapproval. "Like you haven't had enough sweet stuff lately. I saw Grandma sneak you a gingerbread man before we left."

Pooper scooper. I'd have to tell Grandma she needed to be sneakier. "Don't worry, Mom. He wasn't sweet at all. She gave him a mustache, so he was actually a pretty tough gingerbread man."

Mom turned her back on me and continued her inspection of every inch of the store. "Don't make me laugh."

More trudging behind her. "Why not? You haven't laughed much at all lately."

She stopped.

I froze to keep from running into her and knocking her off her crutches.

"I'm sorry, Joey. I'm just so miserable." She turned back toward me and the look on her face made me almost want to cry. "How would you feel if we were up here and you couldn't do anything but hobble around? No skating. No skiing. No dancing whenever your favorite Christmas song came on the radio?"

"Uh … I'd be okay without the dancing."

Her shoulders sagged. "You know what I mean."

I did. Because there would be nothing worse than sitting on the couch and watching everybody else build snowmen and have snowball fights outside without me. It would be even worse than shopping. "I know, Mom.

I'm sorry. I don't know how you …" I stopped as a memory from the gymnastics center hit me. The memory of my favorite coach doing handstand push-ups on the balance beam while wearing a cast on his foot. Mom couldn't do that, but she could do other Mom-type things, like … "Yoga!"

Mom looked down at her legs. "I know. I'm getting tired of wearing these same yoga pants every day, but they're the only thing that are comfortable with this walking boot, and—"

"They're perfect, Mom. You may not be able to wear your dancing shoes, but you can wear your yoga pants and do yoga."

Mom blinked. "I can do yoga?"

I slapped my hands together overhead and lifted a foot toward my knee. "Isn't this the tree pose?" I was truly embarrassed to know this, but the Mommy and Me Yoga Class was the first "activity" Mom ever signed me up for. I also knew that if there was a row of four-year-olds all standing in this position and someone were to push one, they would all fall over like dominoes.

We never went back for a second class.

"Yes." Mom leaned her crutches up against a bookcase that also looked like a tree branch and slowly posed in a similar position. "Oh yeah. I can feel it working. This is great for my core." She smiled.

I smiled back. Boo-yah on the best behavior. Now if only Christine would call with an idea of what Grandma wanted for Christmas.

"Carol of the Bells" played inside Mom's purse. Her purse was the one bag I refused to carry. Thank goodness it had a strap very similar to Chewbacca's bandolier in Star Wars so she could wear it while using crutches.

"I think your phone is ringing," I said with fingers crossed. If Christine was on the phone, my Christmas gift was coming early.

Mom didn't move. She stared at a spot over my head.

"I'll get it for you if you want."

She nodded. Or maybe she just had an itch on her nose. Either way, her head moved. So I figured it would be okay if I retrieved her phone from her purse.

I answered on the second rendition of the song. "Hello?"

"Joey?"

Yes! It was my sister. How weird was it that I was excited to talk to her? "Yep. It's me. What did you find out?"

"It's not good news," she said. "Grandma wants a snowmobile."

Not good news? That was awesome news. I had the coolest grandma in the universe. She put mustaches on her cookies and bred huskies and wanted her own snowmobile. Somehow I'd known that would be the perfect gift.

Oh, wait. I'd already ruled the snowmobile out because it was way over my price range.

"You don't think Mom will loan me enough money to buy her one?" Just in case there was any hope at all.

Silence.

Sigh. "All right. Well, thanks for trying."

More silence.

I guess we weren't used to talking to each other nicely. "See you when I get back."

"Okay."

Click.

The receiver went dead.

Another sound came from outside, a great, roaring, mighty sound.

My heart leaped within my chest. There was still hope. How had I not thought of this before?

It was brilliant. It was beyond brilliant. Christine would have to sing my praises for the rest of our lives over this one.

Outside the window, sparkling in the sunshine,

almost deafening with its power, was a snow blower. The kind that would clear off my grandparents' driveway in minutes.

And no, Grandma couldn't ride it out on the lake, but she could use it to get to her mailbox without having to put on snow boots. It would change her life forever. And it would make up for my horrible snow-shoveling skills.

I probably couldn't get my parents to lend me the money to buy a brand-new one, but I bet I could afford a used one. I clicked on the internet icon on Mom's phone to pull up my gift of choice on Craigslist.

Fifty dollars.

That was enough to make angels sing. It was like another Christmas miracle.

"Mom!"

She had to say yes. She had to lend me the money for a Christmas gift. Dad didn't like to lend me money, but Mom never let anything get in the way of her shopping. She loved wrapping presents. And she would love that I'd thought of the perfect gift for her in-laws. "Mom, can I borrow money to buy a gift for Grandma and Grandpa?"

I had to get her to an ATM.

I reached for the shopping bags I'd set on the ground before remembering that I still had Mom's phone in my

85

hand. I pivoted back to her purse and shoved her phone inside.

"Ack." Mom leaned toward me.

Pooper scooper. I'd shoved too hard. I'd knocked Mom off balance from her tree pose.

I grabbed her crutches. "Here." I jabbed them toward her, hoping she could grip the handles in time. But it wasn't the handles that I should have been worrying about.

The tip of the crutch hit the bookshelf behind her. Books spilled out.

I lunged to catch them and rammed into Mom's one good leg.

Crutches flew one way and she flew another. Right on top of me she flew, flattening me like a snowman pancake.

My face smashed into the musty-smelling books and I left it there. Something told me we wouldn't be doing any more shopping for a while.

Chapter Eight:
Wild Sleigh Ride

Dad wasn't too happy about being called away from his hockey game to drive us back to my grandparents' place. "Now why were you doing yoga in the store again?" he asked Mom.

Somehow I'd gotten out of being punished for this. Maybe Dad figured there was no excuse for me and it was just up to everyone around me to keep me in line. But Mom was already having enough trouble as it was. And it wasn't like Dad could do anything worse to me than take away my snowball launcher.

"It's my fault, Dad," I said from the backseat. "I thought Mom might feel better if she could do something physical, like yoga."

He ran a hand over his face at the stoplight. "In a store?"

"She was already dressed for it."

"It's all right, Joey," Mom said flatly.

But it wasn't all right. Everything just kept getting

87

worse. Mom's injury was awesome at first because she couldn't stop me from eating sugar, but that was half the fun. Like in the Ninja Turtles video game where I was Leonardo and Mom was Shredder. It was more exciting with an opponent.

Then there was Dad, who, for once, had started to look at me with respect in his eyes.

I'd ruined that. Of course.

Christine was getting along with me for the moment, but she wouldn't be when Winston got to take her favorite puppy home with him after Christmas. She'd be sure to blame me for that as well.

I crossed my arms and slouched down in my seat as "Blue Christmas" came on the radio. Fitting.

Dad sighed. "What would cheer you guys up?"

My initial response would normally have been "hot cocoa" or "sugar cookies" but that would probably just put Mom into a deeper funk. "Snowboarding?" I blurted. Oops. That wouldn't work for Mom either.

Mom leaned her head against the window. "You guys can go snowboarding without me. I've already ruined your hockey game, babe. I don't want to ruin anything else."

Dad reached across the seat for her hand.

I pulled my hat down over my eyes so I wouldn't have

to see them get all mushy. If only I had my earbuds with me, I wouldn't have to hear Mom call Dad *babe* again. That was just nasty.

"I want to do something *with* you, sweetheart."

Double bleck.

"Well, there's not much I can actually do."

"I know something."

I perked up. Maybe he would take us to that hot springs with the yurts that I'd been wanting to go to. Mom could do that, couldn't she? And it would be fun to go in the snow. If anybody got too hot, I could always pull out my snowball launcher to cool them off.

"A sleigh ride."

I dropped my head back against the seat. Could winter vacation get any worse that sitting still in a sleigh and looking at nature while squished together with my family?

"I ran into the Lancasters at the hockey game. They booked a sleigh ride for this afternoon. How about I see if we can join them?"

Apparently it could get worse. Not only would I be jammed into the sleigh with my family, but Isabelle would be there too. Next to Winston.

And I'd thought watching Mom and Dad get mushy was bad.

"Please, no," I croaked in my best I'm-dying voice.

But that only made Mom laugh.

And I knew what that meant. If Mom was laughing again, Dad would think he was onto something.

Giddyup.

"No." Dad held up his index finger to show that he meant business—which actually meant no business for me. "You are not bringing your snowball shooter thingy on our sleigh ride. You are not even supposed to have it for the rest of the day."

"But what if we get attacked by elk?" I motioned toward the small, dark dots roaming the snow-covered hills in the distance. They may have looked harmless, but they had us outnumbered for sure. "Who would defend us?"

Dad narrowed his eyes.

"What? It could happen."

Dad reached for my baby.

"Whoa." I whipped the weapon behind my back so that the poor boy wouldn't think I was so willing to hand him over. He'd be better off if I left him on the car seat than for Dad to shove him in the trunk like a kidnapping victim. Not that Dad had ever kidnapped anybody, but my snowball launcher wouldn't know that. "I'll leave him in the car."

"Joey, come here," Mom called from the sleigh where she was petting a couple of really big horses that looked as if they were wearing white socks. "I want to get a picture with you kids and the Clydesdales."

Just what I wanted to remember our vacation by—a photo of me with my scheming cousin and turncoat neighbor. "Really? Do I have to?"

The car door slammed behind me a little too loudly.

I spun around.

Dad crossed his arms. "All right, kid. I know this isn't the most enjoyable event for you, but can you at least not ruin it for your mother?"

Well, since he put it that way. Of course … "I'm not *trying* to ruin it."

"How about you try to enjoy it?" He attempted to lift a brow to look intimidating, but the hat Aunt Polly knitted him must have been a little too tight because the gesture just squished his forehead into a bunch of wrinkles on one side.

I huffed. Why had Dad called me "kid"? Usually he was the one calling me "Joe" as if I were more mature than the winning Winston. Being called "kid" rubbed my

91

insides raw like a rope tow on mittens.

His hand clamped down over my shoulder. "Please, please, behave."

"Sure, Dad," I mumbled. It wouldn't ruin Mom's experience if I slouched in the backseat of the sleigh and kept my mouth quiet by licking my wounds, would it?

Dad tilted his head like maybe he understood the pain of having to spend an afternoon sitting still. "If you can do this for me, son, we'll borrow Grandpa's friend's snowmobile tomorrow."

My chin dropped to my scarf as Dad's words repeated themselves in my head. Snowmobile? Tomorrow? Would I get to drive it? Would Mom try to sign me up for a special snowmobile club if I did? Did it matter? "Gah … psht … ack." I couldn't form the words to thank the most amazing father in the world.

Part of me was afraid that I'd heard him wrong. That if I thanked him for the most outstanding offer ever he'd laugh and say, "Just kidding. You can't even drive a golf cart without ending up in a sand trap. You really think I'd let you run a snowmobile?"

He winked.

I wrapped my arms around him probably hard enough to make him wonder if he was being mauled by one of those bears that got into Grandma and Grandpa's garbage cans. "I will make this the best day of Mom's life," I vowed. "Because you just made this the best day of my life."

"Ha. We'll see."

Yes, he would. I wasn't going to mess up this opportunity. If Dad bribed me with all-terrain vehicles more often, I'd really be the little angel everybody thought Winston was.

Mom motioned to me again.

I gave her my toothpaste-commercial smile. "Coming, Mother."

"Coming, Mother," Winston mimicked me as we both headed toward the horses.

I ignored his smirk. Not even my obnoxious relative could ruin this day, though I did step to the opposite side of the horses from him.

Christine joined me.

I looked down at her in surprise. She must really dislike Winston if she preferred to stand on my side of the horses.

Mom beamed as she balanced on one foot to take our picture with her phone.

If getting along with my sister made Mom that happy, then I'd only just begun. I wrapped my arm around Christine's shoulder.

Angela Ruth Strong

She shook it off.

Oh well. I'd tried. And that's all Dad had asked me to do.

Unfortunately, having Christine on my side of the horses meant Isabelle had more room to join Winston on his side.

"I'm glad we get to go on the sleigh ride with you, Isabelle." He sounded like a dumb prince in some fairy tale.

She giggled.

I rolled my eyes.

"Say 'sleigh bells,'" Mom called.

"Sleigh bells," I said through what was now starting to become a pasted-on smile.

"Perfect."

And it probably was—for her.

I ignored the way Winston helped Isabelle into the sleigh and offered her the hand warmers Grandma gave him. For all I cared, they could jump on the horses and ride off into the sunset together.

Gentle snowflakes fell as the sleigh glided over the smooth surface of the earth. Mom started a round of Christmas carols, and I joined in the loudest. This made Mom happy as well as drowning out Winston and Isabelle's conversation behind me.

When we stopped to feed the elk, the big animals headed toward us as if wanting to order hamburgers in a fast food drive-through.

"Guess what?" I whispered to one as it nibbled on my offering. "Tomorrow I get to drive a snowmobile." If I focused on that, then I wouldn't be bothered by the fact that Winston was helping Isabelle hold out the hay. Or the fact that she didn't need help but only pretended she did so he would sit closer to her.

Gunther, the driver of the sleigh, took my talking to animals to mean that I wanted to know a bunch of facts about them. I made myself listen to him instead of Winston's stupid joke about how snowmen keep their money in a snowbank.

"Only Colorado and Montana have more elk than Idaho." Gunther's thick accent made him a little hard to understand. "They are part of the deer family and can weigh up to 700 pounds and eat up to 15 pounds of food a day."

"That's a lot of hamburgers." I could be as funny as Winston. Or so I'd thought.

Only Gunther chuckled. "These elk are more likely to become a hamburger than to eat a hamburger."

I swallowed hard. "Oh."

Now Isabelle laughed. But at me instead of with me.

"Time to head back down. Would anybody like to have a turn driving my team?"

If it got me away from Isabelle and her new boyfriend? "Oh yeah!" Plus, it was a great chance to prove to Dad that I was capable of driving through snow. The thought of driving a snowmobile tomorrow could get me through anything today.

"May I?" asked Winston.

Grr. Why hadn't Isabelle jumped at the chance? Maybe I should back out so I didn't have to compete with Super Kid.

"Come on up, boys."

Too late now.

Mom squeezed my arm on the way up. "This will make some great pictures."

That's right—I was doing this for her. She liked pictures almost as much as Grandma did. I smiled politely as she snapped another shot of me taking a seat on the front bench between Winston and the driver. I would have preferred to sit on the other side of the driver, but he'd scooted to the edge.

Gunther handed me the reins first. "Hold them tight. No slack."

I pulled back to keep the leather straps from looking like jump ropes.

96

"That's it. Now the other thing you have to do is speak with confidence, let my horses know you are in control."

"Okay." I could do that. It would be just like all those times I told Isabelle how to help out with my last business, except the horses would actually listen.

"We'll start slowly by walking them. Maybe after you get the hang of that, you can tell them to run."

I pressed my lips together to keep from grinning. Nothing like the offer of a little excitement to make me feel better.

"No shenanigans," Dad called.

Of course not. I wouldn't risk it.

"When you're ready, call them by name and tell them to walk."

I sat straight up like one of Santa's elves trying to look taller. On Dasher and Dancer and Prancer and Vixen. "Steve and Billy, walk." I rocked back in my seat as they took the first step forward.

It had worked.

I regained my balance and checked to make sure that the reins stayed taut.

"Nice job, Joey," said my happy mom.

I looked back proudly at Dad.

He nodded approvingly.

Snowmobile, here I come.

"You're amazing." Winston kept his sarcasm under his breath so that only I heard him.

I ignored it. That's what Mom told me to do with bullies. The whole if-you-don't-run-away-they-can't-chase-you kind of thing.

Gunther twisted to share more fun facts with the riders.

I strained to hear what he was saying, but Winston's whisper in my ear drowned him out.

"I tried to tell Isabelle how amazing you are, Joey, but she insisted that you're only good at causing trouble."

I shifted farther away from him. To keep from punching him in the face. "I'm really not." I didn't have to punch him to be able to put him in his place. "I'm being so good today, Dad's going to let me take out a snowmobile tomorrow."

"You think?"

"I know." That was all I had to say. He could just see for himself the next day. I tuned back in to what Gunther was saying about how much weight Steve and Billy could pull.

"Run!" Winston shouted.

Wait. What?

The horses didn't wait. They took off like in a race to

98

our car.

The movement knocked me sideways. I flailed and caught myself instead of falling headfirst to the ground. I dropped the reins, but at least I was still on the sleigh and not upside down with only my feet sticking out of the snow.

Christine screamed behind me. Then there was a thud. And some kind of scrambling.

"Stop!" Dad yelled.

I knelt down and reached for the reins so I could halt the horses.

"Whoa, Steve and Billy!" Gunther shouted.

We all jerked forward again as the horses' hooves stilled. I spun around to make sure everyone was okay. I'd take care of Winston later.

Mom clutched Christine. Dad clutched Mom. Grandpa clutched Grandma. And Mr. Lancaster clutched Mrs. Lancaster, who looked as if she was about to jump out of the sleigh.

But where was Isabelle?

"Isabelle!" Winston called, climbing to the ground.

I followed his line of sight to find Isabelle trying to sit up in the snow. Had she really fallen out of the sleigh?

"Are you okay?" My cousin rushed over to help her stand up.

I waited for her to deck him for his little stunt. Seeing her punch him would be even more satisfying than punching him myself.

"Oh, Winston." She rose and clutched him around his middle and buried her face in his shoulder.

I blinked in confusion. Maybe she was so scared that she'd let anybody comfort her, but in a moment the anger was sure to overcome the fear. I waited.

Her parents jumped down into the snow and raced to her side.

But she stayed hugging Winston.

"Give me the reins, young man."

I handed them over to a scowling Gunther. Why was he scowling at me?

"Josiah Michaels." Mom used her you-better-plan-to-spend-the-rest-of-your-life-grounded voice.

I frowned at her. "What?"

"Your father told you no shenanigans."

"But—"

"Get back here, Joe," said Dad.

I turned and studied his face.

He looked as angry as he sounded.

Did he think I'd told the horses to run? "I didn't—"

"Joey." Winston whirled. "I can't believe you would risk Isabelle's life like that just to have a little fun."

He blamed me? I hadn't done anything. For once, I hadn't done anything. "I wouldn't. I—"

Then Isabelle's eyes met mine. Her sad eyes. She'd never looked at me like that before. Usually if she was angry at me, all I saw was her ponytail after she flipped it in my face. "When you hurt somebody, you should care more about how they feel than defending yourself."

Yeah. Of course. Except I wasn't the one who'd hurt her.

"Do you need my help to climb back in the sleigh?" asked the real culprit.

I, on the other hand, couldn't think of anything to say. If I asked her how she felt now, it would seem phony. If I tried to explain my innocence, she would ignore it. I watched helplessly as she turned away from me and took Winston's hand.

"Joey, come sister by your sit," Grandpa directed in his backwards way before turning to apologize to Gunther about me while my parents calmed down Isabelle's parents.

I didn't argue because I didn't want him to bring up how I had caused him to "snow" in the "slip" earlier that day. He was probably just glad not to be the one to "sleigh" out of the "fall."

I obediently crawled over the front bench into the

101

back of the sleigh and zipped my coat as high as it would go, wishing I could zip it up over my face completely. I'd never wanted to disappear more.

"You should say sorry," Christine said.

I hadn't expected her to stay on my side very long. "I didn't do anything."

"I know, but you could at least say you're sorry she fell. We're all sorry she fell. Except maybe for lover boy over there."

What? Christine believed me when nobody else did? "You heard Winston tell the horses to run?" I asked, ready to break into the "Hallelujah Chorus."

"Yes. He's a sneaky meanie."

"He's a very sneaky meanie."

"You can be a meanie too sometimes, but you're not sneaky about it."

"One of my finest qualities." I nodded. "I can't believe Mom and Dad are falling for his lies."

"They'll figure it out," Christine said. "We never get away with anything. I don't think Winston will, either."

"Will Dad still let me ride a snowmobile tomorrow?"

She burst out laughing.

Yeah, that's what I thought too.

Isabelle's laugh joined my sister's, but when I looked back at my neighbor, it seemed that she was giggling

102

about something Winston had said. My stomach lurched. "Will Isabelle figure it out?"

Christine shrugged. "She's turning into a teenager, and teenage girls are brainless when it comes to boys."

That's what I was afraid of.

Chapter Nine:
Frosty the Snowmobile

The next day Grandma turned our waffles green with food coloring and stacked the little triangles to look like Christmas trees with piped whipped cream for garland and berries for ornaments.

I dipped a huckleberry into the cream and stared at it.

There was no fear of Mom ripping the sugary breakfast out of my hands, as she was on the other side of the room in a yoga pose with both hands on the floor and her casted foot up in the air.

There was no rush at all as breakfast might be the highlight of my day. It's not like I had a snowmobile to ride around or anything.

Christine plopped down next to me. "What's wrong with your berry?"

"Nothing. It's an absolutely incredible berry."

"Are you just bummed that Mom's not going to come over and try to wipe the whipped cream off?"

So she felt it too. "A little bit."

"Would you like me to steal it and eat it?"

I popped the fruit in my mouth. "I'd like to see you try," I said as I chewed. The tart berry burst all over my tongue.

She smiled.

I smiled. Then I realized I was that much closer to finishing my breakfast and having nothing to do for the rest of the day. I slumped back down.

"What's wrong?"

I could go ahead and tell her. She might have sabotaged my hijinks in the past, but now that Winston was picking on me, she'd become my defender. As if nobody was allowed to pick on me but her. "I'd been hoping to go snowmobiling today, remember?"

"Oh yeah." She chewed a berry of her own. "Did you try to tell Dad that the sleigh thing was Winston's fault?"

I lifted one shoulder in a shrug. "He said that since I was the one with the reins in my hand at the time, I should take responsibility."

She scrunched up her face. "That makes as much sense as blaming him for the car wreck that the deer caused on the way up here."

I shrugged both shoulders this time. Though I agreed with my little sister's sudden grasp on logic, I didn't think bringing up the subject of the accident with Dad was

105

going to earn me any Brownie points.

"You could hang out with me and my favorite husky today."

"Thanks." I should probably go back to work to try to make enough money to show Grandma that I was a reliable individual and earn the privilege of taking said puppy home. Though that idea was starting to seem more and more impossible. After the snow-shoveling payback, I still needed forty dollars to buy that snow blower. And even then I didn't know if it would make up for the sidewalk icing and the wild sleigh ride.

"Or …" Christine hopped off her stool and disappeared down the hallway back toward the bedrooms. Was she going to suggest to Dad that I watch a figure-skating show with her? Or sit on Santa's lap? Or something else equally girly and kiddish?

I cut up my green waffles and smeared each piece around in whipped cream before shoveling them into my mouth. I was just about to lick my plate clean when my sister emerged with Dad. As they headed my way, I put the plate down.

"Well." Dad slapped a hand on the counter. "You'll never guess what your sister just told me."

Groan. "She didn't ask if you would take us to see Santa, did she? Because I'm getting a little big for that."

106

"Uh … no."

Christine smacked me on the back of the head.

"Hey."

"You're never too big to sit on Santa's lap." She jutted her chin out.

Well then. I'd been premature on my assumption that she was becoming more logical.

Dad gave Christine his I'm-not-mad-at-you-yet-but-will-be-if-you-do-that-again squinty eyes before focusing back on me. "She told me what Winston did yesterday."

She did what? First of all, Christine would normally be pleased to see me get in trouble. Second, I'd already told Dad what Winston had done. Third, her actions weren't going to matter if Winston was around to argue his way out of this one.

I glanced around the great room.

Only Mom balancing on one foot like she was turning into Karate Kid or something.

"He's back with Grandma being sized for his Joseph costume for the Living Nativity tonight," Dad said, reading my mind the way only parents could.

"So you believe me now?" That was what really mattered.

Dad sighed. "I'm sorry for not believing you earlier. I just want to be careful not to blame Winston for

107

anything he hasn't done. He's going through a tough time right now."

He was going through a tough time? More like he's causing others to have a tough time. "What could be so bad that it's okay for him to get me in trouble?"

"Well …" Dad looked down. "His parents are thinking of getting a divorce."

A snowball might as well have been lobbed at my gut with the force those words had on my digestive system. "Uncle Alex?" Dad would never divorce Mom, so I just figured that his brother wouldn't divorce his wife, either. I mean, I hoped Dad would never divorce Mom.

As crazy as she drove me sometimes with her clean-eating obsession and her happy dancing, I already missed that part of her. And she wasn't gone, just injured.

"Yes." Dad rubbed a hand over his face. "They are trying to work it out, which is why they went on vacation without Winston. But I can tell he feels abandoned."

My eyes got kinda watery, so I blinked until they dried up. "Is that why he's acting like such a punk?" Maybe I could forgive him. It would be easier if my cousin just cried and told us how he was feeling, but if he already felt abandoned by the most important people in his life, he might have trouble trusting those who were less important.

108

"Probably. I've heard it said that the people who are the hardest to love are the people who need it the most."

Made me feel just a little bad about wanting to punch him in the face yesterday. But … "He just gets away with being a liar then?" Mom and Dad said they disciplined me because they loved me, so maybe the best way for them to show Winston they loved him was to ground him. That only seemed fair.

Dad scratched his bald head. "I think maybe the best thing for Winston right now would be for him not to have the power to keep you from going snowmobiling today. What do you think?"

I leaped off my stool and threw my arms up in victory. Then I started kicking my legs and shaking my rump and doing 360-degree jumps.

Mom's happy dancing must be rubbing off on me.

"I take it you agree?"

"Yes, yes, yes-yes-yes!" I pumped a fist in the air with each *yes*.

❄   ❄   ❄   ❄   ❄

I craned my neck to stare out the rear window at the gorgeous snowmobile being pulled behind the truck. For the next two hours, it was all mine. I was the luckiest kid

109

on earth.

Dad slowed to wait for a couple tourists with an orange flag to cross the street. Wouldn't it be cool if I knew them? If they went to my school? And they saw me riding around town with a snowmobile? I bet that would earn me some "cool" points.

The tourists were strangers. But behind them was Micah.

I rolled the window down and leaned out. "Micah!"

The kid turned. His mouth fell open.

I hadn't made it back to snowball fight with him the day before, and he looked like he'd been sitting by the bear statues waiting for me the entire time.

"Micah? Want to go snowmobiling?"

"Yes!" Micah jumped to his feet.

"Joe, get back in here," Dad ordered from behind the steering wheel.

I didn't see what the big deal was—he'd stopped before I'd stuck my head out the window. "Dad, Micah is my employee. He should come with me on the snowmobile trails."

Dad yanked on my jacket so he could roll the window up as Micah jumped in the backseat. He twisted around to see who I'd invited to join us but then had to face forward again as the cars behind us began to honk.

"*You* are Joe's employee?" Dad's eyes flicked toward the rearview mirror again.

Micah smiled as if being employed by a snowball fight professional was equal to a career in the NBA or winning an Oscar for acting or finding a cure for cancer. "Yep."

"Are you two planning to throw snowballs from the snowmobile?" That little wrinkle that Mom usually got when talking to me appeared between Dad's eyebrows.

"That's a great idea, Dad. People will probably pay big bucks to have us do mobile-by snowballings."

Micah rocked with laughter. "I can ride behind you and shoot people with your launcher."

"Oh boy," said Dad, but he smiled. Which he always did when talking about making money. "Micah, do you need my phone to call your parents and get permission?"

"Mom can't talk on the phone at work," Micah said. "But she would be okay with it. She likes it when friends invite me to do things so I'm not just sitting at home. Especially on my vacation days."

Dad glanced over at me.

I smiled brightly to make him think this was still a good idea.

"What about your dad?" Dad asked.

"He moved away."

I peeked over the seat to see if Micah was being

serious. Why would his dad move away? Had his parents divorced like Winston's might?

Micah didn't look up, so I couldn't find any answers in his eyes.

"Oh, that's too bad," my dad said.

I looked at Dad in a new way. What would my life be like without him? When he'd talked about Winston's parents getting a divorce, I'd thought about how much darker life would be without Mom, but I hadn't considered life without a father. A life where Mom would have to get a real job and I'd be the only man in the house to protect her. That would make it really hard to have fun being a kid.

I wanted to share Dad with Micah. I wanted my new friend to be able to have fun for the day.

Dad cleared his throat. "Do you have snow pants, Micah?"

"No, but I could borrow my mom's. She won't need them while she's working." He pointed to a wooden restaurant that kind of reminded me of a saloon in the old west. "Stop there."

"Okay." Dad pulled into the driveway and parked at a funny angle so that the snowmobile we were pulling behind us didn't stick out into the road.

I squinted as we entered the dark foyer, but even

112

before my eyes focused, I could tell the place was packed with families and elderly couples and skiers still half-dressed in their ski clothes. Everyone was yelling to each other over the twang of country music. The smell of sizzling meat almost made me want to delay our snowmobile trip to have an early lunch.

"Mom," Micah called to a woman with a ponytail who raced by while balancing two trays of food in her hands.

She spotted him, but didn't slow her hustle. With a quick spin to place a tray down, she deftly delivered the plates of food on the one then switched trays to distribute the other meals. Just as quickly, she stacked the trays together and headed back our way, calling out acknowledgments to each table she passed.

Her eyes jumped from Micah to Dad to me then Micah again. "Whatcha doin', sugar?"

He beamed. "This is my friend Joey that I told you about. He's the one who paid me to help him make snowballs."

"Right, right." She patted me on the head, glancing over her shoulder toward a window to the kitchen when a bell chimed. "That was real sweet. Are you folks here for lunch?"

"No." Dad extended his hand. "I'm Joe's dad, Tom

113

Michaels, and I wanted to see if it would be okay if I took your son snowmobiling with us today."

Her eyes stilled as she shook Dad's hand. "I'm sure he would love that. Thank you. Thank you so much."

Dad smiled, though the corner of his eyes didn't crinkle up as much as usual. "He said you might have snow pants he could wear."

"Snow pants? I wore them on my walk to work, but he can use them now."

"Regina!" called a man now peeking through the window where steaming plates of food waited for her timely delivery.

"Just a second," she called back, whirling behind the hostess booth. She disappeared underneath it before reappearing with pink snow pants

Dad and I stared in horror. Micah couldn't possibly wear those. Yes, it would keep his legs warm, but it would also get him teased mercilessly.

Her eyes started to shine. She blinked. "It's all I have."

Micah reached for them.

Dad held him back. "If those are your snow pants, we don't want to take them from you, ma'am. I need to get Joe some bigger ones anyway. I'll stop at the store on our way to the trails, and Micah can have Joe's pants. His grandma accidentally got him some that are a size too small."

Thank You, Jesus. It wasn't that I didn't want to be seen with a boy wearing pink, though, I mean, it would lose me some "cool" points. It was that my dad was willing to step in and take care of this kid before Micah even realized he needed it. That's what a real dad did, wasn't it? I was blessed to have a real dad. Which obviously was more than a lot of kids had.

Dad also pulled the hat Aunt Polly made him off his head and handed it to Micah. "It was too tight for my head anyway," he whispered to me under his breath.

"Thank you!" Micah pulled the thing over his shaggy hair.

"Thank you." Micah's mom's chin dropped. "I want to learn to knit so I can make him things like that."

"Regina!" yelled the sweaty face again.

"I've got to go." She leaned forward and kissed Micah's pink cheeks. "You have fun today. I'm so happy for you."

He beamed. "Me too."

Dad and I didn't say anything on our stop at the store, but we didn't have to. Micah talked nonstop about how much he'd always wanted to ride a snowmobile. I'd really wanted to ride one, but that was because I "deserved" it, and I got all pouty when I didn't think I would get to go. That seemed pretty selfish compared to this kid who never imagined he'd ever get to ride one because his mom couldn't even afford to get him snow pants or a hat. I swallowed over the lump in my throat and decided to make Micah's ride an event he would never forget.

The truth was that Micah made the ride incredible. He sat behind me and his laughter seemed to ring out along the peaceful landscape with every turn or bump I took.

"You ready to make some money?" I asked, heading back toward Bear Creek Lodge after our first run. Hopefully I could earn enough cash to buy Grandma the snow blower.

"Totally," he said. "I used that last dollar you gave me to buy Mom a package of toilet paper. She really stresses out when we run out of toilet paper."

I skidded to a stop, sending a wall of snow cascading over a few other snowmobilers. I pivoted to face my new little buddy. "You bought toilet paper?"

His shoulders lifted toward his helmet. "Just a small package. At the dollar store."

I couldn't imagine having to spend my money on such essentials. We ran out of t.p. once when Mom was sick, but we made do with a box of tissues until Dad was

116

able to stop at the store on his way home from work.

"Oh. Let's split today's money in half." The words popped out of my mouth before I could measure their full weight. That meant that if I was going to be able to buy Grandma a snow blower, we'd have to make eighty dollars combined.

Was that possible? Maybe. Was it fair? Yes.

"Seriously?" the kid asked.

As serious as running out of toilet paper. But I didn't say that out loud. "Of course."

A cold spray of snowflakes engulfed us as another snowmobile pulled beside ours. The rider pulled off a blue and silver helmet and long, brown hair cascaded around her shoulders. "Josiah Michaels," Isabelle said without any trace of her damsel-in-distress act. "Are you here hoping to knock me into the snow again today?"

I pulled my helmet off. "I am now." So what if yesterday's fall wasn't my fault? She deserved it. "Only my cousin isn't here to rescue you this time."

She laughed. "Then maybe I'll just stand up for myself."

"Can you?" This was the Isabelle that I used to like hanging out with.

"Wanna find out?"

The only thing that I wanted more was for this

conversation to be recorded so Winston could see that she didn't need him to be her hero. "Micah, do you have the snowball launcher loaded?" I asked as an answer to her question. Business would have to wait.

"Loaded." He clamped the top of the launcher in place to lock the three snowballs in.

"Think you can beat me to the top of the hill without getting knocked of your snowmobile?"

She turned the key in her ignition.

My heart revved like it had an engine of its own. "Ready ..." I gripped my handlebars harder. "Set ..." I positioned my thumb on the throttle. "Go!"

Our vehicle blasted forward alongside hers. Engines roared and wind whipped against my jacket. First we shot ahead, then she charged into the lead as we raced toward the hill in the distance. Not the best position if my goal was to beat her to the top, but perfect if my goal was for Micah to knock her off the machine. He'd have a close target.

"Fire!" I yelled at him.

A snowball whizzed behind Isabelle's back.

That was close, but not close enough. The hill rushed to meet us and before I knew it, we were on the incline. "Aim ahead of her," I called, hoping to help Micah adjust his angle on the launcher.

A second snowball exploded against Isabelle's windshield.

He'd over-corrected. If he could just find that happy medium …

Snowmobilers at the top of the hill stopped to watch us. Helmets came off. Cameras came out. If we put on a good show, this might kick off business for the day.

"One more shot!" I yelled to Micah. "You've got this."

His one-handed grip tightened on my waist as his other arm raised the launcher toward our target. In only a few more seconds, Isabelle might beat us to the top of the hill.

"Now!"

I leaned forward to make us even more aerodynamic. I couldn't focus on Isabelle or Micah. I had to do my best to climb the hill with power. If he got her, he got her. If not, it was up to me to make sure we beat her to the finish line.

"I got her!"

We sailed over the edge of the plateau, and I pulled the handlebars sideways and braked so we could look down the hill at Micah's victory.

Sure enough, Isabelle's machine slowed to a stop since her kill switch had been pulled when she'd sailed into the snow. She sat up and shook her head, exactly like she had the day before. Only this time, she stood, pulled off her helmet, and grinned. "You got lucky," she called.

"Not a chance." I motioned to Micah behind me. "I hired a sharpshooter after you quit on me the other day."

She climbed back on her snowmobile and joined us at the top of the hill to the sound of cheers.

Micah hopped off the back of our snowmobile and headed toward the crowd clapping for him. He'd earned all the glory with his skills.

I let him go.

"I guess I deserved that," Isabelle said, pulling my attention back to her.

She deserved more than a blast with my snowball launcher. I mimicked her from yesterday. "Oh, Winston. I'm so scared. Hug me."

She shrugged. "A girl's gotta do what a girl's gotta do."

I stuck a finger down my throat as if her words made me gag. "And I used to think you were cooler than most girls."

"Then why didn't you want to work with me in our old business anymore?"

"Because you never listened to me."

"Yes, I did. I just didn't agree."

My insides started to boil in that way that can make steam come out my ears. "You never agree."

"You mean the way I agree with Winston?"

"No. That's just stupid."

"You can't have it both ways, Joe. Either I'm the girl that speaks her mind, or I'm the girl that acts mindless."

I narrowed my eyes. She did have a point. The very thing I liked about her was the very thing I didn't like about her.

"Joey, Joey." Micah ran back my way. "I've got more races lined up for us. These other guys want to see if they can beat us up the hill without me knocking them off their snowmobiles. And they are going to pay us five

121

bucks every time we win. Can you believe it? It's the best day of my life!"

Wow. The kid was better at business than I'd expected. And I was glad he was having a great day. I'd thought snowmobiling would also make today the best day of my life, but somehow my talk with Isabelle had soured it. Maybe because she'd been my first business partner, and it didn't seem right to cut her out just because we'd had some disagreements. "Do you want to take turns racing these guys?" I asked her.

Her cheek dimpled. "Nah. I'm headed back to Bear Creek Lodge. Winston is supposed to meet my family there so we can ride out to the hot springs."

The hot springs. So that's why Winston didn't want to come with us today. I'd felt thrilled at the time, but now I was jealous. "Okay." So not okay.

"Ready, Joey? We can beat them. I know we can beat them."

Isabelle rode away as Micah talked. There was just something about her that made me feel more competitive. Which was stupid. Racing a girl my age should not have been nearly as exciting as racing a group of older guys.

I focused as best I could and won eight races. That was pretty good, I guess. Not good enough to buy

Grandma a snow blower, but good enough to keep Micah's mom supplied with t.p. for a while.

I still had one more day to make my last twenty bucks. And no matter what it took, I was going to get Isabelle out of my head and make it happen.

Chapter Ten:
Not So Silent Night

"Do I have to go?" I asked. "I mean, I'm really tired from snowmobiling all day. I think I need to go to bed early."

Mom balanced on her good foot to pull her mittens on. "If you're tired, it's because you haven't had enough good nutrition lately. I can make breakfast in the morning if you think that will help. I have this new recipe for oatmeal."

Mission: Abort.

I grabbed my jacket. "Never mind. I'm feeling my second wind kick in. Besides, I wouldn't want to miss Winston play the role of Joseph in the Living Nativity."

Winston adjusted the pillow case held on his head with a strip of cloth tied around it Rambo-style.

Grandma had improved her costume creations. When I played a shepherd back in kindergarten, she just let me wear the hooded cape from my Anakin Skywalker costume. She thought it worked until the audience started humming the Star Wars theme song when I walked out on stage. And with that kind of encouragement, I couldn't be stopped from using my staff like a light saber. Mom wasn't too happy, but the only problem I had was deciding if Yoda or R2-D2 would make a better baby Jesus in a Star Wars Nativity set.

"You look great, Winston," Mom said.

Moms really didn't have any clue what it meant to look great, did they?

"Thanks." He turned his slimy smile my way. "I'm glad you are coming, Joey. And I'm sure Isabelle is, too. Or should I call her 'Mary'?"

"What?" Isabelle was playing Mary? She was playing Winston's wife? I should have seen that coming. Though I know if I'd agreed to play Joseph, she never would have agreed to the role. "Mom, maybe I do want to go to bed now and eat your souped-up oatmeal in the morning."

"Oh, Joey." Mom huffed. "Give this a chance. You enjoyed my performance at the theater this summer."

Winston laughed.

If I still had my Anakin costume, I would be really tempted to try and use The Force to pin him to the wall. "It's not the same, Mom. I know how this story ends."

"Of course you do. That's the beauty of it. We get to

125

celebrate the ending." Mom spread her arms wide, allowing one crutch to drop to the ground. But that didn't stop her speech. "We have the freedom to celebrate. We have a whole holiday where we get to share this story of the birth of Jesus with people who don't know what it means. We have the chance to see if the story has new meaning for us in the ways we've grown over the past year."

"All right." I wasn't going to argue with that. Though I did wonder how much I'd grown over the past year. Would the birth of Jesus really mean something different to me now?

Winston snorted. "Your mom thinks you've matured?"

I gave Mom my did-you-hear-that eyeballs, but she apparently hadn't.

She was too busy humming Christmas carols to herself. So Winston got away with it again.

I wouldn't get angry. As Dad said, Winston was going through a very tough time. I'd refuse to let his goading get to me. I'd laugh it off. Maybe a joke would help. "What do you call Joseph when he's wearing earmuffs in the Living Nativity?"

Winston looked up toward the star on the Christmas tree as if thinking. Finally, he looked back down.

126

"What?"

"Anything you want because he can't hear you."

He took a step toward me, hands balled into fists. "I won't be wearing earmuffs on stage."

Dude couldn't take a joke. "Good. Because that would just be weird."

He pointed a finger at me. "So you better not be calling me any names."

Christine stepped in front of me, her tinsel halo tickling my nose. "Or what?" she demanded. The girl put the "ha" in hallelujah. She had kept me from getting into a fight with Joseph in front of my grandparents' Christmas tree.

I stepped back and crossed my arms. "Or what?" I repeated. I wasn't going to fight over Winston telling me what I could and couldn't do.

He could talk all he wanted. That didn't mean he had any control.

His face turned the color of a holly berry.

Mom flipped off all the lights in the room except for the white twinkle lights on the Christmas tree. "Let's go, kids," she called, seemingly oblivious to the standoff she was interrupting.

I tilted my head toward the door. The sooner Winston left me alone, the better.

He swiped his staff from the couch and stomped out the door.

"Thanks, sis," I said. She really had become my guardian angel.

She shrugged and knelt next to the kennel to say bye to her favorite pup. "Did you make any money today?" she asked, reminding me what her true goal was in working together.

"Yeah. But I need another twenty. And tomorrow is Christmas Eve. I'm not sure I'm going to make it."

"Are you praying that you will?"

I pressed my lips together instead of answering. Prayer often became my last resort, like a "Hail Mary" play in football. Maybe if I'd prayed in the beginning, I might have avoided some stupid choices along the way, and I wouldn't be in the final hours of desperation.

"I'm praying for you," she said.

I'd never thought of my little sister as praying before. Especially for me. She was always the one that I prayed for God to rescue me from. But now, with her dressed like an angel, I wondered if perhaps God needed to rescue her from me. I was the one who always messed everything up by forgetting to ask for help until it was almost too late.

We tromped through the crunchy snow and climbed

in the backseat of the truck as I contemplated the truce in our relationship. Even if it were still only a matter of having a common goal, I could still thank her for working with me. "Thanks for your prayers."

Dad started the engine of Grandpa's old truck and pulled out onto the street.

Winston leaned around Christine, who sat in the middle, so he could join our private conversation. "What are you praying for?"

That was a dangerous question if I ever heard one. I kept my mouth shut.

Christine didn't. "I'm praying for God to make a way for Joey to earn enough money to buy Grandma a snow blower and show her how responsible he is so Grandma will give him the puppy instead of giving it to you."

I braced for an explosion. I think my parents did too by the way their conversation on the top ten Christmas songs of all time came to a screeching halt.

Seemed "Silent Night" would win by default.

Winston's smile appeared and disappeared with passing street lights. It was the kind of smile that would have had him beating out Jim Carrey for the role of The Grinch.

I shivered.

Dad cleared his throat. "I'm not sure if that's how

prayer works, Christine. I don't think God honors prayers that are going to hurt other people. Usually it's better if you pray for God's will to be done."

Christine adjusted her halo. "Can I pray for the best man to win?"

Winston's smile slipped, and when it reappeared, I'm pretty sure his teeth were grinding.

Dad gave a nervous laugh. "God pretty much promises that. Everybody reaps what they sow. It doesn't always happen as quickly as we would like it to, so we just have to trust in Him and ask for guidance in how to sow the best seeds possible."

Christine nodded, though her expression stayed blank.

"To sow means to plant, and to reap means harvest," I said. "So, for example, if you plant kindness, you get kindness in return."

Her eyebrows lifted in understanding. "Got it."

"Or …" Winston somehow tilted his head without letting the smile slip off. "If you plant meanness, you get meanness in return."

Mom and Dad's profiles turned toward each other for just a moment. They were probably wondering if Winston was trying to help Christine grasp the concept or if he was making a threat.

Once we arrived at the church, I opened my door, hopped out as quickly as possible, and ushered Christine into the dressing room and away from Mr. Meanness.

As soon as she saw the other angels, she started oohing and aahing over their costumes and begging them to share their glitter makeup. She obviously didn't need me anymore.

I spun to go find my seat with my family. I found my neighbor instead.

She stood there in a long, blue robe with her wavy hair down.

"Nice … uh … baby doll." Argh. I meant to tell her that she looked nice.

She wrinkled her nose. "At least it won't spit up on me like my cousin did this morning."

The image made me smile. "Sounds more enjoyable than hanging out with *my* cousin."

Her eyes lost their sparkle. "You know he's going through a lot, right?"

"Yes." I knew. That's why he was getting away with being such a punk. But I was done walking on eggshells around him. It was time he reaped what he had sown. One more sneaky act of cruelty and he was going to get it. Big time.

"Five minutes," called the director to all the actors.

That was my cue to leave. It wasn't like my conversation with Isabelle could get any more awkward anyway. "Gotta go."

An all too familiar screech came from behind me. "My halo. Has anybody seen my halo?"

If Christine's halo was missing, I knew exactly where to look. I zeroed in on Winston as the rest of the crew circled around my little sister.

Winston edged backward toward a trash can. His eyes caught mine just as a sparkly, gold, round thing slipped from the sleeve of his oversized robe and into the garbage. Talk about a trick up his sleeve. Could he be any more cliché?

I stalked over. He wasn't getting away with this one.

"Winston!" called the director. "I need all the leading actors to take their places."

He winked at me before strutting away.

Fine. But after the performance, I was definitely telling my parents what he'd done. For now, I'd have to settle with getting Christine's crown back. I leaned over the garbage can and retrieved her bent halo. I smoothed and reshaped it the best I could.

"Joe?" Isabelle's baby doll hung limply from her hand. "What are you doing with that? Christine needs her halo to go on stage in one minute." Her nostrils flared. Not good.

Christine jogged over, tears in her eyes. "Thank you." she said.

She knew the truth. And she'd stand up for me when it counted. But, for now, I had to let her go fly onto stage and proclaim the good news. "You're welcome. Just watch out for—"

Applause drowned out the rest of my warning as Winston stepped onto the stage.

I should have been out there with my family, but instead, I was still behind the curtain. Christine was fine now. I could go join them. I headed for the door.

Winston reappeared as the angels started to file out onto the stage.

I ignored him and waved at Christine.

She smiled and waved.

For just a moment, I saw her as a cute little girl and not the snotty little brat I usually considered her to be. This weird kind of pride welled inside me. The kind that didn't even make sense because it wasn't like her cuteness made me a better person or anything. But maybe it was that recognizing her cuteness made me better. Maybe I *had* grown since last Christmas when I laughed at her for messing up the line of her solo in the school choir performance, though it was pretty funny how she sang "Barney's the king of Israel" instead of "Born is the King of Israel" in "The First Noel."

She turned back to go through the curtain.

Winston stuck a foot out in front of her.

I didn't see her fall, but a thud came from on stage and the crowd gasped. My little sister could have just truly broken a leg. I waited for the cry.

A patter of feet and swish of a robe. "Halo there," she said in greeting.

The crowd roared with laughter.

And my sister went from being just another angel to being the star of the show. She must take after my mother in that department.

"Good try," I said to Winston.

He shrugged his arms in innocence, but only because Isabelle was watching.

She sent me a look that read *come on*. "Will you lay off already? Why would Winston want to trip your sister?"

I could have told her. I could have explained the whole puppy thing. But that would have sounded pretty stupid. I'd just get him later. A little snowball action was sure to chill him out.

Except ... I didn't have to wait for later. What if I did to him what he did to Christine? But with a snowball. Down the back of his robe as he walked onto stage. Yeah. See if he could come out of that situation as shining as Christine had.

"I'll just go ..." I tilted my head toward the door instead of finishing the sentence. Because Isabelle probably would have tried to stop me had I actually said the words "outside to make a snowball."

The full moon made the snow glow.

I packed a handful together.

Cold. Hard. And just wet enough.

I waited, peeking through the door until Winston's brown robe and white pillowcase moved toward the curtains. I'd have to be fast to get to him before he went out on stage, but at least nobody would see me coming

135

that way.

There he was. With a couple of other characters. The curtains parted and they headed out in a line.

I charged forward. He'd almost disappeared, but I reached through the curtains and grabbed his collar just in time. The snow slipped from my fingers.

He howled.

The snowball must have gotten hung up at the belt around his waist. Either he'd have to finish the scene in agony or he'd start jumping around to get rid of the icy chunk, making a huge, embarrassing scene.

Another howl. Stamping feet.

Other cast members asked what he was doing, and mutters came from the audience.

I covered my mouth and turned my head to keep from laughing out loud. My laughter died a sudden and horrible death because standing next to me was an incredibly calm Winston.

While the kid I thought was Winston caused chaos out on the stage.

"Oh no."

Winston's lips turned up. He stuck a thumb toward the stage. "Did you think that was me?"

"Oh no," I repeated.

"Because it's not."

The commotion grew louder. The curtains swung wildly as if the poor kid couldn't find the opening.

The least I could do was help him get off stage. I reached through the curtains to show him the way, but it was too late.

With a mighty rip, one whole side of the curtains came crashing to the ground.

And there I stood, staring out at the audience as if I were the only one on stage.

Chapter Eleven:
The Fight before Christmas

Oatmeal for breakfast. And Grandma didn't even smuggle me any Red Hots to put in it. Not much chance of her giving me a puppy anymore—not after my act that brought down the house—literally—last night.

Winston stirred his hot cocoa with a peppermint stick across the breakfast bar from me. "Want some?"

"Joey doesn't need any sugar," Mom answered for me from her latest yoga pose in the living room, just as Winston knew she would.

Christine joined me at the counter, saw the oatmeal, and retreated. "What are we doing today, Mommy?"

No response. Nobody would ever guess by the crankiness in the cabin that today was Christmas Eve.

It was supposed to be a magical day. A day of wonder and anticipation. Instead, all I felt was dread. Mom and Dad hadn't yet given me my punishment for the night before. Maybe they'd been too shocked to respond. So now, possibilities hung over my head like a raincloud at a parade.

Would I have to go shopping with Mom a second time? I doubted she would want that. Would I have to write apology letters to every one of the kids in the Living Nativity last night? My hand cramped at the idea. Such a task could keep me from ever throwing a snowball again. Or maybe they'd just have the poor shepherd that I'd assaulted last night stick snow down my shirt as payback. That wouldn't be so bad.

Dad came out of the bedroom. "Joe, you are going to volunteer your time to wrap presents today. All the money you make will go to the church drama team for next year's Christmas production."

I slumped back against my stool and stared at the wood-planked ceiling. Not gift-wrapping—the exact opposite of what every twelve-year-old boy wants to do. Especially while on vacation in a winter wonderland.

"Don't argue." Dad warned.

I wanted to say, "I'm not arguing," but that might have sounded too much like arguing. So I kept my mouth shut. And one hour later, I found myself at a table outside the holiday gift bazaar. Which was definitely bizarre.

At first, happy grandmas brought me girlie-smelling, little bags called sachets and hand-knit scarves and

139

stained glass for me to wrap. But after I accidentally dropped a piece of stained glass, I didn't get as many happy customers. Only panicked men brought me their last minute gifts to wrap.

I stared at a big guy's wooden picture frame in dismay before cutting a piece of snowman paper to size. If only the wooden frame I'd made Grandma hadn't floated down the Payette River, then I wouldn't be in this mess. I wouldn't have had to work to make money for a new gift to prove myself responsible and win the puppy, and Christine wouldn't have prayed for Winston to lose. Then he wouldn't have tripped her as she went out on stage, and I wouldn't have tried to get revenge.

I taped all the corners of the paper to the center of the frame then turned it over so my customer couldn't see the tape and stuck a silver bow on top. "Here."

The man nodded his approval. "Nice."

Isabelle appeared next, making a face that would more likely get her a part in a Halloween movie than a Christmas pageant. "Nice? You call that a wrap job?"

I shrugged. There was probably a reason middle school boys didn't often work at the gift-wrap table.

A man with a jar of jelly appeared behind her. "How much to wrap this?"

I cringed. Breaking stained glass had been messy

140

enough. If I dropped a glass jar with jelly, I'd probably ruin all the wrapping paper we had.

"Two dollars," Isabelle answered. She held out her hand and took the jelly.

I watched as she rolled it in some sparkly silver paper then twisted the extra paper at the tip and tied it with some blue, curly ribbon. "You're good at that."

"I know." She motioned for me to stand up so she could take my chair.

"I can't leave. This is my punishment for last night."

She looked away for a moment. "I'll take your punishment. It's my fault," she finally said.

My mouth fell open. "What do you mean?"

She played with her braid. "It's my fault you hate Winston. I shouldn't have spent so much time with him. I just wanted you to see that some boys do like hanging out with me."

I covered my mouth with a hand to hide my smile. She'd wanted to make me jealous? It hadn't worked at all. Well, maybe just a little. But … "That's not why I tried to stick snow down his robe."

She tilted her head. "It's not?"

"No. I figured you would find out what a punk he was eventually."

She narrowed her eyes. "What do you mean he's a

141

punk?"

How could she not know? "He tripped Christine last night. And he's the one who caused you to fall off the sleigh. He's been using my taste for trouble to blame everything on me."

She crossed her arms. "Are you serious?"

"It doesn't matter anymore." I'd decided not to let it eat at me. I had to spend the rest of Christmas Eve wrapping presents, and I just wasn't going to think about how he got to spend the day.

"Joe, causing trouble isn't the only thing you are good at."

I bit my lip. "Sometimes it seems that way."

She pointed out the window toward the field by the lake. "Winston is out there having snowball fights right now. If there is anything you can beat him at, it's that. I'll finish wrapping presents for you—since I'll make more money at it anyway—and you go put on the biggest Yukigassen tournament of the year."

Was she for real? My fingers itched at the idea. We'd been in McCall almost a whole week and I hadn't had an actual snowball fight with anybody. Besides the sheer joy of waging a winter war, I could charge money for kids to enter the tournament. I could make the money I needed to buy Grandma a snow blower.

But wait. Why would Isabelle wrap presents instead of getting in on the action herself? If she'd been this helpful in our business transactions, we never would have parted ways. "You're not going to leave this table to come join the tournament, are you? Not that I don't want you on my team, but I'm kind of responsible for the present-wrapping."

She grabbed my arm and pulled me up. "I've got you covered."

"Why?"

"Because that's what partners do."

Partners. "You want half my earnings, don't you?"

"Nope." She reached past me for a beaded jewelry set that the lady behind me wanted wrapped. "I just want to work with you again. Merry Christmas, Joe."

This was almost too good to be true. I considered pinching myself, but chose to live the dream instead. "Thank you, partner," I yelled back as I raced out the door.

Micah sat at the base of the bear statue, making snowballs. He looked up from underneath my dad's old hat. "I was hoping you would come, Joey."

Okay, just because Isabelle was my partner again, that didn't mean I could ditch the kid. He was a hard worker. And deserving of every cent I paid him. "We're putting

143

on a Yukigassen tournament."

"We're what?"

I didn't have time to explain. With it being Christmas Eve and all, parents were bound to pick up kids earlier than usual. I leaped up on the bear statue to fill everyone in on the sport at once. "Who knows what Yukigassen is?" I yelled.

Faces turned my way but nobody responded.

"It's a snowball fight. Kind of like dodge ball. Someday it will be in the Olympics. For now, it's the coolest thing to do on Christmas Eve in McCall." I punched an arm in the air to add a little excitement.

Still no response.

I'd have to make it a limited offer. Make the kids compete just to be involved. Let's see, I needed another twenty bucks, so if I charged one dollar per kid and I was splitting my earnings with Micah, we'd need a total of forty kids. "I'm putting on a tournament right now. It's one dollar per registration, and I'm only accepting the first twenty kids per team. Who's in?"

Blank stares. Nobody moved.

Then one kid in a rainbow-striped knit hat stepped forward. Winston. "I'm in. You're going down, Joey. Who's going to help me out?"

A group of younger kids surrounded my cousin,

144

jumping up to give him high fives. They followed him in my direction then broke off to ask their parents for money.

He handed me my first dollar of the day. "I get to throw snowballs at you and see you get in trouble again for not doing what you're supposed to be doing right now? Christmas doesn't get any merrier than this."

I grinned at him. What would he think if he knew his little girlfriend was now on my side, covering my shift at the gift-wrap station so I could kick his tail? "I appreciate your enthusiasm."

Christine appeared beside me. "Yes, we both appreciate your enthusiasm." She whipped open a leather notebook with a pine cone clasp. "I'll sign the kids up, you take the money."

I'd never been more proud of my little sister. And I'd never realized how much I enjoyed being on a team. Even if we had all come together for different reasons, we could better fulfill our purposes by working as one. Isabelle wanted to be business partners again, Micah wanted to make money to buy his mother toilet paper, Christine wanted me to be able to take home the puppy, and I just wanted to put my cousin in his place.

Our team grew by eighteen more kids. Christine agreed to serve as the official, so it was Micah, me, and

145

other younger kids who would actually do the fighting. We started with thirty minutes to build up our half of the field with snow forts and snow bricks and snow walls to hide behind during the game. Once Christine started the time, anybody hit with a snowball would be out. Whichever team had the last man standing got to take home the trophy, which was just a supersized pine cone which I'd named the "Supersized Pine Cone of Superior Performance." Who wouldn't want such a prize?

"Players, on your marks," called Christine.

The tournament would soon be under way.

We huddled behind the fort at the back of our half of the field.

My heart hammered, toes curled, and fingers shook. "You guys can do this," I told my team. "Run fast. Stay low. And take cover before you start throwing snowballs."

The pre-packed snowballs were all in the center of the field. Whichever team got there first would have the most ammunition.

"Get set!" Christine's voice was the only noise on the snow-blanketed field.

I peeked up over the fort to gauge my opponents' positions.

A few bright jackets hovered around their retainer

wall.

"Aim for color."

"Play ball!" Christine ordered.

We charged forward. Directly toward the snowballs.

I scooped up a pile and dove for cover. Unfortunately, my smaller teammates didn't make it in time. Three got hit immediately.

"Out!" Christine would call, pointing back and forth between our teams. So far, numbers remained even.

I poked my head up to find a target and fired.

Out. Out. Out. Not a snowball wasted.

A kid in a red coat fell next to me as a snowball hit him in the chest.

"Out!"

Pooper scooper. "Nice try. Keep practicing and join me again next year."

He groaned and crawled away.

Who had hit him? I peeked over my wall.

Winston nailed another one of my teammates, spotted me, and shot a snowball in my direction.

I ducked just in time.

If I was going to win, Winston had to be stopped.

I army-crawled forward to get a better angle on his hiding place, but he must have done the same thing. Our hiding spots on opposite sides of the field brought us directly across from each other.

He pulled back his arm and lobbed a snowball my direction.

I rolled out of the way, but the kid in front of me didn't see it coming.

Direct hit.

"Out!" called Christine.

Micah scampered over. "I'm going for more snowballs," he whispered.

"But I'm not sure they're out of ammo yet."

"That could work well for us. If they come out of hiding to hit me, then you can hit them."

"You're going to sacrifice yourself?" I asked, shocked and a little in awe of his willingness to take one for the team.

"It makes sense. If you can get a bunch of them out when they are all trying to get me, we can win."

A nice strategy. I just wished it didn't have to be Micah who'd get taken out. Of course, Micah was the only kid willing to do such a thing. "Whenever you're ready."

"I'll try to get some more snowballs back here to you before I'm out."

If anybody could do it, he could. "That would be incredible."

Then he was off. Zig-zagging from wall to wall.

Who would pop out of hiding to throw a snowball at him?

First, the kid with the glasses.

Got him.

Then the kid with the University of Idaho Vandals stocking cap.

I would have hit him anyway just for supporting Boise State's rival.

Then the chubby kid who might someday have a growth spurt and become a superstar athlete. At the moment, though, he moved pretty slowly and his strong suit seemed to be comedy, judging by his dramatic flail backwards from a snowball to the forehead.

"Out! Out! Out!"

Just like Micah had planned. And I'd gotten each of his predators before they got him, so he was still alive. Maybe he'd make it back to me with all those snowballs in his arms. Maybe we could run this play repeatedly until we won.

Assassin number four?

Oops. I'd celebrated too early. I should have been watching for more danger.

Winston launched a ball while flying sideways from one hiding spot to the next.

149

I grabbed my last snowball and fired, but I was too late.

Winston's snowball hit Micah directly in the back and he fell forward, landing a couple feet shy of my ice block.

The snowballs in his arms rolled from his grip toward me.

"Out!"

"So close, dude."

He nodded and climbed to his feet, hands in the air in surrender. "Get him for me, Joey," he said before trudging away.

I would. I had to. Because I was the only player left. And it was Micah's self-sacrifice that had saved me.

"It's just you and me, Joey," yelled Winston.

That was good news and bad news. The good news was that I didn't have to worry about anybody else. The bad news was that if I lost, then it would be because Winston beat me. Again.

Isabelle's words rang through my head. *Winston is out there having snowball fights right now. If there is anything you can beat him at, it's that.*

I couldn't beat him at snow shoveling. I couldn't beat him at behaving. I couldn't beat him at winning a popularity vote. But I could beat him at a snowball fight.

Why? Because it was my calling, my future. And all of

my past training had led me up to this moment.

My study of Yukigassen. My water-balloon throwing. My gymnastics classes. It all came together to form a plan.

"Joey?" Mom's voice called.

My time was up. I couldn't hide out any longer. I had to win this now so I could respond to my mother and hopefully not spend Christmas Day grounded to the bedroom.

"Joe?" Dad's voice. They must have both discovered I wasn't wrapping presents anymore.

Winston laughed. It was his Joker laugh. The kind that grated against my nerves every time. Except this time it gave away his location.

I scooped up snowballs and took a deep breath. Time to put my plan into action. I started with a dive roll behind another wall, popping up to toss a snowball his direction. Then a log roll behind a block even closer to his hiding place where I tossed another snowball to keep him in hiding. I finished with a back roll to the very snow brick he cowered behind, leaped to my feet, and jumped over the wall, both arms cocked back.

Splat. Splat.

I got him both times.

My team cheered and ran out on the field to congratulate me.

Winston gawked. "N-not fair," he stammered. "You can't come on my side of the field."

That had never been a rule. Beating a kid who changed the rules would normally affect my satisfaction, but not today. Not with a group of kids surrounding me and chanting my name.

"Jo-ey, Jo-ey!"

Christine pushed her way through the crowd to join me on the wall. She raised the Supersized Pine Cone of Superior Performance above our heads. "And the winner is Joey Michaels on Team Joey!"

I did it. I'd won. I'd finally beaten my cousin.

Winston shook the snow off his arms. He snorted. "It doesn't matter if you won, Joey. You're still going to be in trouble with your parents."

He did have a point. I waved over at Mom and Dad, hoping Isabelle had explained that she'd offered to wrap gifts for me.

They frowned at the kids all slapping me on the back and knocking knuckles with each other.

I left the celebration behind to trudge through the snow toward them.

Would it help to pray?

Father God, don't let me be in trouble again.

A scripture verse from Sunday School popped into my head. The one about how God disciplines those He loves like a father disciplines his child. Not the answer I was hoping for.

I thought back to Dad's lesson the night before on prayer. Dad really did love me and want the best for me. I'd be doing myself a favor if I listened to him once in a while.

Father God, please let Your will be done.

"What's going on?" Dad asked.

"Yukigassen."

"And you won?" Mom sounded more proud than

153

mad.

Dad shot her a look he usually reserved for me.

She sobered.

"I did win." I tried to hide my smile. Because no matter how good it felt to beat the winning Winston, that's not why I'd started the competition in the first place. "More importantly, I've raised enough money to buy Grandma a used snow blower for Christmas. Would you guys take me to pick it up so I can give it to her tomorrow?"

Dad's eyebrows shot toward his bare, bald head. "You earned that much money?"

"Actually more, but I split it with Micah." I waved at my new friend who had made my Yukigassen win possible.

He must have thought I was waving him over. He charged our way with a smile and my dad's old hat. "Merry Christmas!" he gushed to my parents. "This is the best Christmas ever. I can actually buy my mom a turkey for dinner tomorrow."

We all stared. Micah's mom didn't have money to buy her own Christmas dinner? My parents might have been momentarily impressed with my thoughtfulness for Grandma, but that was nothing compared with the kid who was going to give all he had so that his mom might have something the rest of us took for granted.

Dad rubbed his face. "Does your mom have the day off tomorrow?"

"Yep!"

My parents looked at each other. I knew what they were thinking.

Especially my mother who was so incredibly concerned with diet. "Maybe you guys could join us for dinner, then."

"Really?" Micah clapped his supersized gloves together.

From now on, I would think of them as the Supersized Gloves of Superior Performance because I'd never met anybody else so happy and willing to work. That was the kind of performance that mattered in life, wasn't it?

I looked down at my pine cone. I could give it to him. He deserved it. And he would be happy with it. But it wouldn't make as much difference in his life as the money in my pocket would.

"We'd love to have you over," said Mom. "Then maybe you could use the money you made to buy yourself a special treat. Like a candy cane or some fudge."

My mom just suggested a kid buy himself candy? She

must really be feeling bad for Micah.

"Oh, I couldn't do that," said Micah. "Mom works so hard to take care of me. I'd want to help her out. I'll put the money in her stocking so she can pay the electric bill and keep the heat on."

Whoa. My dad complained about electric bills, but I'd never worried about him not paying them. I didn't realize it could be such a big deal to turn on a light or toast bread.

I swallowed over the lump in my throat as a thought formed in my mind. It wasn't a normal thought for me. There were no competitions or reckless behavior involved. In fact, this thought involved me shoveling the walkway for Grandma and Grandpa for the rest of our stay in McCall. It also involved giving up my hope of getting a husky for Christmas.

I dug fifty dollars out of my pocket. "You know what, Micah?" I said. "You really earned this money today. I wouldn't have won without you. Merry Christmas."

His eyes widened. And got a little shiny.

And I was afraid that if I looked into them any longer, they would make my eyes get shiny too.

So shiny they would even leak a little.

I shoved it toward him. "Take it."

His oversized gloves had trouble holding onto the

cash.

I had to get away so I could stop thinking about how little all that money would really do for him.

Mom spent more than that on my gymnastics classes every month. Would Micah ever be able to play sports?

"I'll see you tomorrow," I said before running across the crosswalk back toward the church where Mom and Dad had parked. Hopefully we'd be going back to the cabin soon. I was suddenly more tired than I had been the night before.

Chapter Twelve:
We Wish You a Furry Christmas

Christine shook my bed the next morning. "Grandma put pretzel antlers on chocolate donuts to make them look like reindeer," she whispered to wake me up.

Chocolate donuts for breakfast? I didn't even know that was legal.

I swung my feet over the edge of the bed and rubbed my eyes. This was the morning I'd waited for all year. And usually it was because I was excited about opening my presents, but today the excitement was because I knew my friend Micah would get to open presents.

After I'd given him all my money yesterday, Mom and Dad had gone over to the grill and bar to make sure Micah and his mom would join us for Christmas dinner, then we had all gone shopping to get them stuff from the store. McCall was a little town, so there wasn't a big selection, but I'd actually been able to find Micah his own snowball launcher.

"Let's go see if there is a puppy in your stocking,"

Christine whispered.

I grabbed her arm to keep her from running out of the room. Did she not know? Had I forgotten to tell her yesterday? "I didn't buy Grandma the snow blower."

I could barely see her forehead wrinkle in the silver, early morning light. "What? You made all that money in the Yukigassen tournament, though." She stuck her hands on her hips. "You didn't decide to buy yourself an arctic snow shield instead, did you?"

Hardly. "No. I gave the money to Micah. To help his mom pay their heat bill."

Her hands dropped to her sides. "You have to pay for heat?"

I shrugged. "I guess."

"Oh." She clasped her hands together. "Well, that was really nice of you."

I shrugged again.

"But that means Winston is going to get the puppy, doesn't it?"

I nodded. "Probably."

She wiped at a tear. "At least we have heat."

Normally I called her a baby when she cried, but this time I felt a little bad for her. Like I had chosen to give Micah heat instead of earn the husky for her.

She was being very brave. And it would help if we

159

could focus on the positive. Like if we compared ourselves to the kid who had nothing rather than the kid who won everything. "And we have chocolate donuts."

She sniffed. "I can play with the puppies one more week, too. Some kids don't even get to play with pets at all."

I wondered if that was really true. Were there kids out there who never got to play with animals? Probably. And Micah might be one of them. I'd show him the puppies when he came over later today.

We sneaked out to the kitchen and made ourselves hot cocoa to drink with our donuts before Mom got up and forced herbal tea down our throats. Then we sat in the glow of the Christmas tree as long as we could before turning on some really loud Christmas music to wake everybody else up.

It was a great morning. And not just because I got my arctic snow shield, which I put next to my snowball blaster so they could get to know each other.

Grandma came out of the mud room holding a puppy with a red ribbon tied around its neck.

I glanced guiltily at Christine then over at Winston who was sitting up even straighter than normal. He'd done it. He'd totally fooled the adults into thinking he was a responsible young man.

160

"As you all know"—Grandma lifted the fur ball in her arms—"there is a puppy in my litter that is a little smaller than the others. People who want to buy a husky aren't going to want to pay for him. So I told Winston I was going to give him to one of you children—the one I thought showed the most responsibility."

Christine chewed a fingernail. Did she still think I had a shot at having Grandma consider me responsible? I had run around outside in my underwear the first day we'd spent here, for goodness' sake.

"The puppy goes to …"

I blew air up toward my hair. The suspense was only going to make it harder for my little sis. I hope she didn't spend the rest of the day crying in her room while Winston got to play with his new pup.

"Christine."

What?

"What?" She jumped to her feet.

Grandma handed her the husky. "While these boys were outside trying to outdo each other, you were the one inside taking care of him. You've earned the puppy, Christine."

She did cry then. But happy tears. The only kind that should ever be cried on Christmas. "My own puppy? I have my very own puppy?"

161

The joy was contagious. Mom and Dad and I laughed at her delight.

"Well played, Grandma," I said.

Winston jumped to his feet. "Not well played at all. How could you?"

I leaned forward in shock. My cousin had let his mask slip off. Now everybody got to see the kid I'd dealt with.

"I gave you that mechanical dog feeder you wanted. I bought it with my own money. And you didn't even give me the puppy?"

I looked away, almost embarrassed for him. Even though he'd been a punk to me all week, I would have rather he truly became the kid he pretended to be than to turn on everyone else.

Grandpa stepped in front of Grandma. "I told you to be fun and have good. Maybe you should listen next time, sonny."

Winston glared. Which was really ridiculous because his pile of gifts was bigger than any of ours. I think it was because everybody felt a little sorry for him and wanted him to enjoy the season, even without his parents. But what would ever be enough for Winston? Even if he'd gotten the puppy, he wouldn't be cuddling it the way Christine was. He'd be rubbing it in all of our faces, demanding Grandma take him to the store to buy dog food and chew toys.

The doorbell chimed.

We all relaxed a little from the distraction.

Saved by the bell. But who could it be? Micah and his mother weren't due for another hour or so.

Grandpa hobbled over to the door and swung it open.

Outside stood Uncle Alex and Aunt Polly. They were smiling.

"Mom! Dad!" Winston ran to them like Christine ran to her puppy. "What are you doing here?" he asked between hugs and laughter and happy tears.

"We missed you, son. I know these past few months have been really hard on you. So we are going to work really hard to keep our family together," Winston's dad said.

Aunt Polly nodded. "Neither of us can imagine not having you in our home all the time. We're so sorry that we left you at Christmas. You deserve more than this from us."

It was too bad Micah couldn't have his parents reunite for Christmas, but I'd prayed for God's will to be done, and my parents had stepped in to help Micah's mom out. Maybe that was how family worked. When one person stepped out, God brought another person to

163

step in. That way we were never left alone. We were never abandoned.

Dad put an arm around me and an arm around Christine. Mom hopped over on one foot to join our own family hug.

Christine's husky wiggled and climbed up on her shoulders to take turns licking all our faces.

I'd hoped we'd be taking the little fluff ball home with us, but I'd never imagined it would happen this way. "Welcome to our crazy family, little guy."

"Snowball." Christine reached up to pet her pup's fur. "I'm going to name him Snowball in your honor, Joey."

I laughed. "Really? Because I stuck a snowball down a shepherd's robe to defend your honor?"

"That is pretty memorable. But that wasn't the only snowball you threw this year."

Mom and Dad joined in the laughter. Then Grandpa and Grandma. Then Winston and his parents.

This wasn't the Christmas any of us had planned, but because of the challenges, we'd grown closer as a family. Kind of like teammates in a game of Yukigassen. It took some sacrifice. Yet in the end, we got to celebrate the victory *together*.

Merry Christmas to all, and to all a good fight!

The End

Dear Reader,

Christmas is magical, but it can also be a tough time for families. It can feel like we are being forced to love people we don't even like. That's how it was for Joey anyway. As for Winston and Micah, the people they loved—parents—weren't there for them.

The truth is that oftentimes grownups don't even realize *connection* is a choice. We all have the ability to create relationships with those around us if we want to. And when we choose *connection*, we become stronger than we were on our own.

If other people choose to *disconnect* with us, that's their choice. For example, it wasn't Winston's fault his parents were thinking about getting a divorce, and it wasn't Joey's fault Winston was picking on him. Sometimes when people hurt on the inside, they make poor choices that cause us pain. That's when we have the choice to keep sharing that pain (like how Joey tried to get Winston back by putting the snowball down his robe) or to move on (the way Micah did by helping out his mom).

So maybe this season, don't focus on what you want from other people but on what you have to offer them. Maybe that's where the magic of the holidays comes from—from choosing to put aside our own feelings and *connect* with others.

And you can always *connect* more with me at www.angelaruthstrong.com or by writing to angelaruthstrong@gmail.com.

Merry Christmas and happy snowball fighting,

Angela

Meet the Author

Angela Ruth Strong didn't run businesses as a kid, but in 7th grade she did start her own neighborhood newspaper. This childhood interest led to studying journalism at the University of Oregon and having one of her stories reach over half a million readers. To help other aspiring authors, Angela founded IDAhope Writers in Boise, Idaho, where she currently lives with her husband and three children, who always love a good snowball fight.

Acknowledgments

Jack and Geri, for bringing family together at their cabin in McCall where some of our most beautiful memories were made.

Mike, Ginger, Ellis, and Luanna, for rocking the role of grandparent.

Emily, Josiah, and Chrissi, for a crazy-fun childhood and for letting me name characters after them.

Jordan, Caitlin, and Lauren, for teaching me so much through the ups and downs and joys of parenting.

Johnathan, Ashley, and Kristina, for giving me a chance despite my failures.

Jim, for being willing to do it all again.

Ashberry Lane and my agent, Alice, for making publishing feel like family.

Read the First Book in the Fun4Hire Series Now!

The Water Fight Professional

I, **Joey Michaels**, am the Water Fight Professional.

Basically this means that customers pay me to soak other people. But my super-competitive best friend is sucking all the fun out of summer. All because I made a secret bet with him.

Winning the bet wouldn't be so hard if I didn't have the following three problems:

1) My dramatic mother who feels the need to schedule every moment of summer

2) A surfer-dude mailman who can't keep deliveries straight

3) The annoying neighbor girl who all my friends have a crush on

If I lose … ugh, I can't even tell you what I'd have to do. I'd rather lick a slug!

ASHBERRY
LANE

ASHBERRYLANE.COM

Want to be notified of when

The Food Fight Professional,

Book 3 in the Fun4Hire Series, releases?
Sign up at www.ashberrylane.com.

CPSIA information can be obtained at www.ICGtesting.com
Printed in the USA
LVOW10s2149280715

448036LV00001B/1/P